Fabien's arm was around her waist

His long fingers seemed to burn through the fabric of her dress. If she turned, their mouths would be at kissing distance, but she kept her face obstinately turned aside.

"But I am interested," she said. "Climbing mountains is a subject that interests me very much."

"Some other time, perhaps," he told her. Taking her face in his hand, he turned her toward him. Before she could stop him, his lips were upon hers, and she was swept up in a deep, long kiss.

"Much more interesting than the subject of mountains, Sophie, don't you agree?"

He slipped the shoestring strap off her shoulder and gently cupped the curve of her breast. She sensed his power and was greatly tempted to forget all about the story and submit to the enchantment of this blue day. . . .

Gwen Westwood confesses that, true to romance tradition, she and her future husband began their relationship with an argument. But later, while she was still at university in England, she received a registered parcel containing a beautiful diamond ring that he'd sent from South Africa. "It was to be returned there—with me," she recalls. They were married the day after her ship arrived, and Gwen and her husband with their young family were to see much of the country that would one day enrich the backgrounds of her many fine romance novels.

Books by Gwen Westwood

Bitter Deception

Gwen Westwood

Harlequin Books

TORONTO • NEW YORK • LONDON
AMSTERDAM • PARIS • SYDNEY • HAMBURG
STOCKHOLM • ATHENS • TOKYO • MILAN

Original hardcover edition published in 1987
by Mills & Boon Limited

ISBN 0-373-02885-7

Harlequin Romance first edition January 1988

CHAPTER ONE

So this was the cottage that Sophie had driven so many
miles to see, expertly guiding her little Renault car from
Cherbourg, across the valley of the Loire, through small
towns, past old houses, their wrought-iron balconies
dripping swags of wistaria in shades of lavender and
purple. She, who usually had to hurry to an important
assignment, had given herself the unusual treat of a more
leisurely journey by secondary roads, but all the time
pressing on through country that had become more rugged
as she came nearer to the mountains with panoramas of
valleys and villages of stone, always with a little church, its
bell hung high and exposed in the steeple.

Now here she was at last, really arrived at Les Cerisiers,
and it was more beautiful than the rather blurred
photographs, sent to her by the *notaire*, had promised. Those
pictures had not succeeded in showing its true colours. The
walls had that beautiful shade of rusty gold that seemed to
be a reflection of the years this small house had stood in the
balmy warmth of the southern sun, and they seemed to
glow underneath the sheltering tiles that were the faded
pink of an old-fashioned rose. It hardly mattered that the
waist-high nettles had overgrown the land around the
house or that the lavender, herb-bushes and asparagus fern
were now running wild where they had once presumably
stood regimented in rows.

'For I can soon get that fixed up,' Sophie told herself.
'But, oh, just look at those cherry-trees!'

All around the house, blossom foamed in a creamy sea.

'It's fantastically early,' Sophie said to herself. 'But this is
very far south, almost on the Spanish border. The cherries
could be ripe as early as May, I expect.'

But she would not be here to appreciate them. A month. That was all her editor had allowed her to put her house in order. Even so, she hardly thought he would have willingly given her this time off if it hadn't been that he saw there might be some advantage in it for his journal.

Sophie worked as a writer for one of the most popular journals, one that was considered expert at informing its readers about the intimate details of the lives of celebrities. Lately they had specialised in running a series on what had happened to formerly well-known figures who had dropped out from the public view. Sophie was a valued member of the team that was responsible for these popular features, and, when she asked for time off to go and see the cottage and small-holding she had unexpectedly inherited from an aged uncle, the editor, Mike Kingsford, had been most reluctant to let her have leave.

'I was relying on you, Sophie, to get under the defences of that actor who won awards way back and is rumoured to be considering making a come-back, but until something has been decided he still refuses to give interviews. There's no one else as persuasive as you, Sophie. Must be something to do with that copper-red hair and those innocent big blue eyes. To look at you no one would believe that you can be tough as old shoe leather on occasions.'

'Thank you. No one can turn a compliment into an insult better than you, Mike,' Sophie told him. 'Incidentally, while I'm here, could I have a look at your big wall map of France to trace my route to Les Cerisiers?'

'Sure, help yourself. Where did you say this hovel is that you have inherited from your long-lost uncle?'

'It's not a hovel. At least I hope not, though the *notaire* who wrote to me did say it's in need of some repairs. It's what is known in that part of France as a *mas*, a kind of small-holding with some land around it.'

'So where is this place?'

'Very far south, not far from the Spanish border. The nearest big town is Perpignan, but its nearest small place is

Ceret, the place known for its cherry orchards. It's in the foothills of the Pyrenees.'

'Interesting. That seems to ring a bell. What am I reminded of? Hold on. Let's look at the map. It might give us a clue.'

Sophie looked with some alarm at her editor. His slate-grey eyes were alert but thoughtful, and his long nose quivered like that of a hound that has just got the scent of a desirable fox. She knew that look of old. But it has nothing to do with me, she thought defiantly. I'm taking leave to look at my cottage, and I certainly deserve some time off after the way he has pushed me lately.

'You say this place is not far from Ceret? Ah, yes, here it is. Of course. That's what I was reminded of. The Château de Cressac. It must be quite near to where you will be.'

'Yes, of course, it's right there. The *notaire* mentioned in his letter that the *mas* used to belong to the owner of the château until he sold it to my uncle. The Comte and he were old friends, but he died long ago and I don't know who lives there now.'

'Ah, but I do.'

There was something in her editor's expression that Sophie recognised of old. The expression of an old pressman who scents a good story.

'My dear Sophie, don't you know who the present Comte is?'

'No, why should I? I can hardly expect the family in the château will take much notice of me during the time I'll be there. I'll be far too busy fixing up the *mas* to do any socialising.'

'Not too busy to get a good story, I hope. Your neighbour happens to be Fabien de Cressac. Surely you must have heard of him?'

'Did he have something to do with climbing mountains?'

'Of course, it was probably before your time. I tend to forget how young you are. You were probably still at school when the disaster happened.'

'What was that?'

'He was a man with a glamorous life-style, one of those guys who seem to have everything. Came from a noble old French family, but spent his life organising expeditions into wild places and having different adventures such as round-the-world yacht races, travels in darkest Africa, that sort of thing, but then he became obsessed with mountains and led climbing expeditions all over the world. He was enormously successful until he attempted the north wall of the Eiger. It's one of the most gruelling climbs in the world, and once started there's no going back. Even experienced guides refuse to go to the help of anyone who gets into difficulties there. The conditions can change drastically within half a day. Unexpectedly bad weather with high winds caught them on the face. His three companions were killed and he was badly injured, but with phenomenal strength of will he managed to drag himself back to base at Kleine Scheidegg. His injuries put paid to his climbing days and the death of his friends appeared to affect him badly, though he refused to give interviews or tell his story, so inevitably rumours rose that he had been at fault.

'He gave up the jet-set life he had previously led and became something of a recluse by all accounts in this remote château he had inherited from his father. No one seems to know what has happened to him. It could be of interest to find out, especially if you could persuade him to part with the story of what took place on the Eiger.'

Sophie saw her chance to get some more time to deal with the *mas*.

'I can do that, but I would need more time to get to know him, and, if he's a recluse as you suggest, it might not be easy.'

'I don't expect it will be. After the event no one ever succeeded in getting the true story of what happened. Even before that the media were never very popular with him. He fell foul of the popular press because the emphasis was all on his love-life, making him out to be some kind of Casanova.'

'And was he?'

'Well, undoubtedly he was very attractive to women. So look out for yourself, Sophie.'

'Sounds promising,' Sophie told him. 'But don't worry about me, Mike. I've had plenty of experience at looking after myself. It will take more than a charismatic ex-mountaineer to prise me away from my present life. I'm quite satisfied with that at the moment, thank you, always provided you grant me an extra two weeks to get to know my subject better, as well as the two you owe me.'

Yes, she loved her life as a writer for this well-known journal, and, after making the mistake of falling in love in her extreme youth with a man for whom marriage was impossible, she had opted for a life free of such complications. Maybe some day ... but at the moment she was happy to live her own interesting, exhilarating life.

Now to see in what condition she would find her cottage. She had ideas of spending vacations here, in utter peace far away from the rat-race of the city, and maybe some day she could get sufficient leave to come here and write that book she had always promised herself she would do. At other times, if she could get the house fixed up in a reasonable condition, she could supplement her income by letting it to other people. It was in a good place for vacations, she thought, not too far from the sea and yet within reach of the mountains, and the sun shone for hours every day.

Sophie got out of her car and marched resolutely towards the house picking her way through the tangled weeds and brambles that spread themselves over the path. That old pool, encrusted with last autumn's rotted leaves, could it possibly be made into a swimming place? But first things first. It was the house that needed attention, she thought, as she climbed the broken stones of the steps and stood on the dusty threshold. As she tried to turn the huge key in the rusty lock, a bird flew shouting out of the eaves and a large

spider seemed to gaze malevolently down at her from a
huge web slung across the lintel.

Strange, there seemed to be something wrong with the
lock. How aggravating. Had she been given the wrong
key? But there couldn't be two like this. It was so huge and
old. No wonder it was difficult to work. She put the key in
the lock again and gave the door a mighty push. Much to
her surprise, it gave way immediately, swinging with
practically no noise at all over the old tiled floor of the
entrance. Sophie paused, rather puzzled by the ease with
which she had now gained entry. Of couse, that was it. The
door had not even been locked. She had been locking it and
then trying to open it. How stupid. But then why had the
door been left open? M. Dupont, the *notaire*, had seemed
rather a fussy, pernickety kind of man, a typical man of
law. Who could have left the place unlocked? But there
could be very little left here that was worth stealing
anyway.

She had found herself in a large living-room with rough
walls, grimy with the smoke of many fires that must have
been burned in that large open fireplace with its cast-iron
equipment for an extremely old-fashioned kind of cooking,
including a large spit on which one could roast a huge joint,
even a whole lamb or sucking pig maybe. It would be
lovely to have a log fire during the short months of winter
here, when the cold winds were blowing down from the
mountains, and Canigou, that peak that dominated this
whole valley, was covered in snow.

Maybe one day she could invite her friends here, have a
house party when everything had been fixed up to her own
satisfaction. For a few moments in her imagination the
room was filled with the sound of voices, the clatter of
knives against plates, the bell-like tinkle of wine glasses, the
fragrant smell of garlic and olive oil and herbs, the golden
soft glow of oil lamps and the leaping flames from great
faggots of oak.

But now she was back again in the present and her heart

sank a little as she realised how far away from that dream she was. These floor tiles, they must have been beautiful once but it was difficult to tell what the original colour had been because they were encrusted with dirt, dried mud and dead leaves that must have blown in through that window where the broken shutters banged in the wind.

Of course the house had been empty for some months. It had taken quite a while for all the business side of her inheritance to be cleared up. In fact it was still not all completely organised. She would have to get on to M. Dupont about this matter of the pictures. Her uncle was supposed to have left her some unsold paintings, but so far, the *notaire* had informed her, he had not found them in the house. It was sad that Aristide's pictures had attracted notice only just before he died. She had been told they could be quite valuable now.

If she was to spend vacations here and hope to let it to other people, she would have to buy some more furniture. Evidently Aristide had made do with very little. She had seen photographs of him in his peasant's smock and black beret and now she could imagine how he could have sat at that heavy oak table, that was scarred with much use, possibly sharing a bottle of wine with friends or serving them with a vegetable potage, ladling it into those deeply golden pottery bowls that stood on the shelves of the battered dresser. They would have mopped it up with hunks of the long baguettes purchased fresh every morning. She imagined Aristide walking into the village, when the sun was rising over the low scrub-scented hills that surrounded this property, to buy his bread, and thought that one day she might do the same.

M. Dupont had told her that Aristide had made some improvements to the original peasant's cottage when he had come to live here. There was a wooden stairway leading up to the two bedrooms in the roof and he had installed a bathroom with a shower. She would be glad of that after the long tiring journey, although now she

remembered the *notaire* had told her that, in order to obtain
hot water, one had to light a wood fire under an ancient
geyser. All that would have to be changed eventually and it
would all cost money, but she would think about that later.

The first priority was to bring in her light belongings
and to have a shower, but she would light a fire first in the
living-room, for there were actually logs with paper set in
the big open fireplace. Although it was warm during the
day, the evenings were still chilly in this part of France and
it would be good, when she had showered and changed, to
sit down and drink the red wine she had purchased and
make a salad to eat with the onion and cheese quiche she
had bought at the *charcuterie* that she had passed on the way.

The bathroom and main bedroom were downstairs and,
as she brought her baggage into the room, she was
astonished to see that the room was almost filled with the
most magnificent bed she had ever seen, an ancient piece of
furniture, possibly Empire period, intricately carved with
garlanded flowers held by winged cupids and bare-
breasted goddesses, and festooned with embroidered
curtains in yellow damask. Wherever could this have come
from? It looked more in keeping with a château than this
humble place. Maybe that was it. Perhaps when Aristide
had been friendly with the late Comte de Cressac he had
purchased this magnificent object from his friend. Or could
it be that it had only been borrowed and she would have to
give it back? She would have to ask M. Dupont about that.

Well, she would use it until she found out whether the de
Cressac family had any claim to it. In spite of the beautiful
hangings and feather-soft mattress, the blankets on the bed
were old and thin, so it was a good thing that she had
brought her own duvet filled with goose-down, for she had
not imagined Aristide had cared much about his physical
comfort, and it seemed she was right. She had better make
use of that ancient copper warming-pan that was hanging
on the wall of the living-room in order to air the bed, but
just for tonight she might even sleep in her sleeping-bag in

front of the fire and organise things better tomorrow. Now
the first consideration was to have that shower.

She found a towel from her light nylon pack-bag,
stripped off her jeans and T-shirt in the bedroom and went
into the shower-room next door. It was comparatively
clean and in good order. After she had removed a couple of
spiders by flinging them through the window, she turned
the tap and found that the spring water was still running,
soft and not too cold after the first gasp-making chill.
Coming out of the shower cubicle, she seized the large rose-
coloured towel she had brought, feeling thankful that she
had not economised on the size of this in her otherwise
scanty baggage. It enveloped her in its soft warm folds and
she felt tinglingly good as she dried herself, beginning to be
hungry and looking forward with relish to that supper in
front of the fire, the first meal at Les Cerisiers.

What was that? Once the noise of the gushing water
from the shower had stopped, the quiet of the place had
been broken only by a late blackbird singing his heart out
from the top of a cherry tree. Yet now, from the rooms she
had not yet explored, came a noise and it sounded distinctly
like some person walking overhead. Now the noise stopped.
Sophie was annoyed to find that her heart was beating
quickly, seeming to make a noise as loud as that one she
thought she had just heard. But this was nonsense. She
mustn't start imagining things just because she was not used
to being in such an isolated place. There must be all kinds of
strange noises going on in such an old dwelling. Could it
have been a bird on the roof? Or even a cat? But cats were
soft-footed. They didn't make noises like that. Now she
could hear a kind of rustling. Perhaps there was a rat there.
It would be no wonder because the house had been empty
for so long.

Her heart had just started to slow down and she was
regaining her confidence when she heard the sound again.
This time there could be no mistaking it. Someone was
coming down the stairs. No bird or cat or rat could make a

noise like that. What was she to do now? She hadn't any clothes in which to face this intruder. They were all scattered in the other room. But what was this person doing in her house? Suddenly her fear vanished and she felt nothing but indignation that her peaceful arrival was to be broken up by some irritating intruder. If she went into the bedroom quickly, she thought, she could get into her jeans and T-shirt before she needed to confront whoever was there.

With that, well wrapped in her towel, she opened the swinging slatted door of the shower-room and went swiftly into the bedroom. It was dark in here because the wooden shutters were still fastened across the window and, after the lightness of the bathroom, everything looked black. Groping her way to the bed where she had recently left her clothes, she felt herself seized from behind and two strong arms hurled her to the floor, then she was pinned down and a fierce voice shouted, '*Maintenant, vous êtes attrapé,*'—now you are caught. The hands that had seized her were brutally demanding and she started to struggle, forgetting in her anxiety to escape that she was only wearing a towel. Suddenly the fierce voice changed.

'*Mon Dieu,*' it exclaimed. '*Mais vous êtes une femme.*'

'Yes, I am,' cried Sophie indignantly. 'Of course I am a woman. Who did you think I was, and what are you doing here in my house?'

She heard some muttered imprecation and in the gloom she felt him release her and stride towards the window.

'Don't open the shutters,' she implored.

She quickly gathered the towel around her and, feeling her knees give way, she collapsed upon the bed. Then she heard the sound of a match being struck and the soft glow of an oil lamp illumined the room. She was sitting crouched on the bed, her back pressing against the carved cupids, her knees bent, her hands clutching at the towel that was draped around her leaving her shoulders bare.

The man, standing there in the golden glow of the lamp,

looking curiously at her, was dark and rugged, his eyes black, the sweep of his brow so dark they were positively satanic, his teeth white in contrast to the dark glitter of his smile.

'*Eh bien*, you must be Mademoiselle Brown,' he said. '*Enchanté de vous voir.*'

'Well, I'm not enchanted to see *you*,' Sophie responded crossly but with as much dignity as she could muster considering her present state of undress. 'Who are you and what are you doing in my house?'

'Fabien de Cressac, *mademoiselle*, your nearest neighbour. I did not know you had arrived. My keeper reported that he thought someone had been staying here during the last week. I expect that was you, *mademoiselle*?'

'No, no, I have only just arrived.'

This was a piece of good fortune, thought Sophie, the elusive Comte de Cressac right here, but she was in no state to conduct one of her penetrating interviews.

'Odd, then it seems there might have been someone else living here. When I heard sounds I thought I had caught the intruder.'

'And you tackled me as if you were playing rugby,' Sophie accused him.

'You must pardon me, *mademoiselle*. I must admit I have never had such a pleasant encounter in any rugby match I ever played.'

'I guess not, and must you keep calling me *mademoiselle*?' demanded Sophie irritably. 'My name is Sophie. You may as well call me that.'

'Then you may call me Fabien,' he said graciously.

He smiled and came across to her and, as she drew back, he put his hand under her chin, raising her flushed face until she had to look into those dark eyes. In them there seemed to be a small flickering flame or was that the effect of the lamplight? He seemed to be studying her intently.

'Charming,' he said.

Oh, no you don't, she thought. Mike had warned her that

he used to be considered something of a womaniser, and the effect of that long, strong brown hand under her chin and now smoothing the silky lower half of her face was anything but distasteful. She shrugged away from him and yet she must not appear to want to reject him if she was to get the interview that her editor had demanded.

'Thank you for coming to see about this intruder,' she said, trying to sound more gracious. 'Perhaps you would like to share the wine I have left in the other room. But now I must get dressed and make myself a little more respectable.'

'*Quel dommage.* What a pity. That towel is most becoming. However, dress quickly and you can tell me about yourself over that glass of wine.'

It was he, Fabien de Cressac, who must tell her about himself, thought Sophie. This was going to be easier than she had anticipated, but she wouldn't let him know she was a journalist. He might run away if she did that. No, she must deal with him very carefully if she wanted to get that personal profile.

With hands that she was annoyed to find were trembling a little, Sophie selected a leisure suit in velour with a deep cowl neckline. It was of a vivid hyacinth blue that exactly matched her eyes and enhanced the brilliant lights in her red-gold hair. If Fabien had not come, she supposed she would have just dressed in her jeans and T-shirt, but she must make a good impression if she was to get to know him better.

He had drawn Aristide's old sofa up to the fire and had placed two glasses on a small table and opened the wine, almost, she thought, as if he owned the place and she was his guest. He had also disposed the quiche and croissants upon the rough Breton pottery plates and now seemed in the process of mixing the salad.

'I didn't realise Frenchmen could be so domesticated,' Sophie remarked.

'Do you know a great deal about Frenchmen?' he asked.

'Not as much as I'd like to,' she answered.

And that's quite true, she thought, but it was not all Frenchmen she wished to analyse, only him for her journal.

'*Eh bien*, after such a provocative statement, we must do something about that.'

According to Mike, this man was supposed to be something of a recluse, thought Sophie, yet he hardly seemed to be much of a hermit when it came to chatting up strange women. He was not the kind of type she would go for. From this little acquaintance she decided he seemed far too sure of his own irresistible charm, but she must go along with that for the present. She couldn't afford to offend him if she hoped to get that feature for the journal.

When he had finished tossing the salad to his satisfaction, he came towards her and carefully poured two glasses of wine from the bottle, handling it as if it had been of some rare vintage instead of the very inexpensive wine she had bought from the local grocer. As he came to sit beside her and handed her the glass, she noticed that he seemed to have a slight limp, and at the same time she was conscious of his dark eyes studying her minutely and the shape of his lips that were parted in a rather mocking smile. He was so close to her now that she could see how the little tendrils of hair were tangled in a gold chain upon the muscles of his chest that showed dark bronze against the chalk white of his open shirt.

As she buttered the crusty slices of the baguette and sliced the quiche, she thought that she had hardly expected company on her first night here. But this had solved the problem of how she was to introduce herself to him. She need not let him know yet that she was a journalist. Oh, no, it would be better if before that she should try to find out as much as possible about him without disclosing that she had a purpose in getting to know him better.

'Have you lived here long?' she asked him.

'For a good part of my life. I was born here but went away to school in England. My father, the *Comte*, had some foolish idea that the English public-school system was best.'

'And didn't you think so?'

'Not particularly. I have always been, how would you say, a bit of a rebel. That kind of discipline hardly suited my temperament. However all those cold showers and early risings prepared me for similar hardship in my future life.'

'That sounds formidable. May I ask what your future life was to be?'

As if she didn't know, thought Sophie.

'Let's say that's all in the past. What do the English say? Water under the bridge. That's quite enough about me. Tell me now why you have come here.'

'Why, to have a look at the house, of course.'

'Ah yes, it was left to you by the good Aristide. What a pity that his pictures became popular so late in life. And now you have come, what do you think of your inheritance?'

'It's much more beautiful than I ever imagined.'

'*Mon Dieu*, do you really think so? Are you serious?'

His glance seemed to take in the shabby appearance of the room, the smoke-stained walls, the broken floor-tiles. Sophie felt the hurt of a parent whose much-loved offspring has been criticised.

'Oh, I know it is in a very poor state at the moment, but I'll get it right, you'll see. If I can find good workmen I can get them going during the month I hope to be here, and later I may be able to commute here to see how things are going. It will soon be in good order, I promise you.'

Please take that mocking expression off your face, she wanted to add.

'My dear child, you cannot realise the difficulties you face. You, a young Englishwoman employing French workmen to do renovations in your absence.'

'I'm not a dear child,' Sophie declared. 'I'm a working woman and I only have a month to get things arranged here but I hope to do a lot in that time, the replacing of tiles, the mending of the roof, the modernisation of the plumbing and anything else that needs doing.'

'I hope you have capital for all this. Building is anything but cheap here.'

'I have a little money to go on with and Aristide left me the remainder of his paintings. They're fetching a good price now. I'm sure he wouldn't mind if I used the money to renovate the house.'

'And what do you intend to do with the house when you have managed to renovate it?'

'Spend some lovely long vacations here. Invite my friends. Rent it to other friends. That way I'll get back some of the money I have to spend on it.'

'Wouldn't it be much simpler to sell the place? It's a long way from England. It would be much less expensive to hire someone else's villa when you need one.'

'You don't understand. I love the idea of this place. I have always adored France and this gives me a chance to feel myself a small part of it.'

'So. What do you know of this part of France?'

'Very little,' she admitted. 'But I'd like to know more.'

'It's hardly Paris here, you know.'

'I don't expect it,' she said.

'To one who has come from London, it must have very little sophistication.'

Why is he trying to put me off? she wondered. Is he afraid I might invade his privacy?

'It's a place of very old traditions, right at the extreme end of France, the French Catalonia where another language is spoken as well as French, just as I believe you have in Wales. This is the Roussillon with one foot in the sea and the other in the mountains. There's too much to be learned here in a mere month's vacation.'

'At least I can try,' Sophie protested.

'But why spoil the first evening of your vacation by being too serious? You will find out about your inheritance soon enough and, when you know more about it, you will know how best to deal with it.'

He stood up and stretched himself like a lazy tiger and on his face there was a small secretive smile. She was too conscious of his great height towering over her and she stood up too, feeling herself at a disadvantage.

Outside night had fallen, and inside this room with its glowing fire and leaping shadows seemed like some primitive cave, isolated, hundreds of miles from the outside world. As she met the dark glance of his eyes, Sophie thought that here she seemed completely cut off from her normal life, that life in which she was a well-known and super-efficient journalist. How quiet it seemed here. A burning log shifted and crackled in the fire, and, somewhere in a corner of the room, a cricket began a piercingly shrill, sweet song. From outside came the plaintive calls of owls.

His hands came up and grasped her shoulders. Through the sensuous feel of the velour, they seemed to burn into her flesh.

'You have most beautiful eyes, Sophie,' he murmured. 'Blue as the Mediterranean on a clear day in spring.'

For a moment she felt herself compelled by that hypnotic gaze, but then, all at once, breaking the quiet out there in the darkness, there came the sound of a car's engine silencing the owls with its clamour, and then the noise stopped but was followed by the raucous noise of a klaxon. The spell that had seemed to hold her was broken and, with a muttered oath, Fabien strode across to the door and flung it open as high heels clattered upon the paving stones.

'Rosine, what are you doing here?' he shouted in French.

There followed a stream of French so fast that Sophie could not follow it and into the room came Fabien, his arm around the driver of the car. Sophie thought she was the most beautiful girl she had ever seen. Enormous eyes shone like green emeralds and a waterfall of shining black hair cascaded around a perfect heart-shaped face. She was wearing a suit of winter-white corduroy with narrowly tapered trousers and a blouson jacket that showed off to perfection her tall, slender figure.

'Rosine, meet Sophie. No doubt you recall she is now the owner of Les Cerisiers.'

'*Enchantée*,' Rosine smiled, showing perfect teeth.

'I have two aunts, Germaine and Belle, who keep house for me at the château. They knew I had been told of an intruder here and were worried that I had stayed away so long. *Mon Dieu*, they are like mother hens sometimes. They phoned Rosine thinking I might be there and she came to investigate. Very courageous of you, Rosine, considering there might have been some kind of villain here.'

Rosine gave a small gesture, waving away any suggestion of her bravery.

'But, Fabien, as soon as the aunts told me, I simply had to come. Look, I even brought a small pistol with me in case I needed it.'

In her hand was a dainty pearl-handled weapon.

Fabien grinned.

'Fortunately no need for that, but I appreciate the gesture. What a woman you are, Rosine. The intruder, whoever he was, seems to have vanished, however, and instead I found Sophie here who has come from England to inspect the place.'

'*Eh bien*, Sophie—may I call you that? You and Fabien seem to have made yourselves very cosy.'

It must look rather an intimate scene, Sophie thought, with the remains of the meal, the wine-bottle, the two glasses on the table and the sofa drawn up before the glowing fire in the hearth.

'Would you like a glass of wine?' she asked Rosine. 'I think there is still some left.'

'*Non, merci*, some other time perhaps. We must get back, *chéri*. Germaine and Belle are anxious about you. Poor darlings, they cannot forget your accident and when you go missing they make too much fuss.'

In those few seconds, Fabien's expression seemed to have

changed completely, Sophie observed. The charming smile
he had been directing first to one woman and then the other
had vanished as if a dark cloud had gone over the sun.

'You are right, Rosine. Their anxiety for my welfare can
be very tedious. Unfortunately in my present circumstances it has to be tolerated.'

'*N'importe.* When you are able to rebuild this house, you
will have a place for yourself, a retreat where you can be
alone, but I hope you will often want my company.'

Surely, thought Sophie, she must have misunderstood.
Rosine was speaking in French and it was always difficult
to follow the accent of a person you had never heard before.
Fabien said something quickly and rather sharply in
French to Rosine. Sophie thought his colour had height-
ened but perhaps that was on account of the fire. Rosine
however did not look in the least taken aback.

'You have not spoken to her then of your plan?' she asked
Fabien. 'But I feel sure she will be agreeable. After all,
where else will she find someone to offer her so much money
for a such a ruin?'

'Be careful, Rosine. Sophie understands some French.'

'Why should I be careful, *chéri*? Surely since you are her
neighbour she should give you first refusal on the *mas*?
After all it should have come to you. It was only through
your father the old *Comte's* generosity that Aristide was able
to buy it and at such a low price too.'

Turning to Sophie now, Rosine said in English with a
rather knowing laugh, 'The old *Comte* sometimes used this
house as a *pied à terre* for his many mistresses. Oh, yes, he was
a man of considerable charm and virility. It was only in
later years after he had had a hunting accident that he
decided to let his old friend have it for—how do you say it
in English?—for a song. It was too bad of Aristide not to
will it back to Fabien, for really he is the rightful owner,
n'est-ce pas?'

Sophie thought she had grasped the most essential fact in
Rosine's rather jumbled story.

'Does Rosine mean that you were thinking you might buy Les Cerisiers?' she demanded of Fabien.

Fabien laughed, flinging his hands out in a very French gesture.

'The idea had crossed my mind that you might wish to sell this place. I had no notion that you might consider living here for part of the year.'

'She wants to live here?' exclaimed Rosine. 'But that surely is impossible.'

So that was why he had been so charming to her, thought Sophie. He wanted to get on the right side of her so she would give him first refusal on the *mas*. Just as she had been nice to him, she thought a little guiltily, so that she could get that interview.

'Why should it be impossible?' she demanded of Rosine.

'You are English, aren't you? Why should you want to live here?'

'Sophie has ideas of turning this into a house where tourists could spend vacations.'

'*Bonne Mère*, what an idea! This is not tourist country. It is way off the tourist route. If you want to do that kind of thing, you should buy a villa on the coast.'

'But I own *this* villa,' said Sophie obstinately. 'And I know plenty of people who would be glad to come here, who would appreciate a place where they could find solitude and peace of mind.'

'I don't understand you,' Rosine protested. 'People who come on vacation don't want to be at a place like this. They want amusement and discos. That's what I would want.'

'Not all people are like that.'

'Anyhow, Fabien wouldn't like it to have a villa for tourists right on his grounds.'

That's too bad, thought Sophie. At the moment she didn't feel too concerned about what Fabien might like or dislike.

'Anyway, Fabien needs this place. He has all kinds of plans to improve it, haven't you, *chéri*?'

Fabien didn't reply. Rather surprisingly he seemed willing to let Rosine run on in this way, but perhaps he was pleased to have her expressing his own thoughts.

'I too have plans to improve the place, Rosine, and it so happens that I am the one who has inherited it,' Sophie told her.

Rosine seemed quite oblivious of the anger in Sophie's voice. She shrugged her shoulders.

'*N'importe*. That's not of much importance. I think you will find it is far too expensive and difficult to get building done here when you know so little of the customs and language of this country. When you have found this out, as you soon will, you will be only too pleased to sell it to Fabien. I'm sure he will offer you a most generous price.'

'Leave it, Rosine. Sophie has had a long journey and is doubtless not in a good mood to discuss business. We'll talk about it some other time. I hope you will come over to have *déjeuner* with us tomorrow, Sophie. The aunts will be curious to meet you. They knew Aristide well and were very fond of him.'

'Thank you, I should like that,' Sophie replied.

This was turning out better than she had hoped in spite of Rosine's revelations about Fabien's plans for the *mas*. If she could write that interview, it would help to pay for some of the improvements she hoped to make.

'Come along, Rosine, we had better go home to reassure Germaine and Belle that I have not been kidnapped. *Au revoir*, Sophie, and thank you for your hospitality.'

'*Au revoir*, Sophie, and do think over what we have been saying,' said Rosine, her hands clinging possessively to Fabien's arm. 'I'm sure you will find it better to sell the *mas*. What possible amusement could there be for you in the life we have here? After all, it did belong to the old *Comte* in the first place and it seems only right that his son should have it once more. I'm sure you must agree when you have considered it well.'

So the old *Comte* was reputed to keep his mistresses here, thought Sophie, as she watched the lights of Rosine's car disappearing down the rough track. She supposed that accounted for that splendid bed and wondered if Fabien wanted it for the same reason. Or for just one mistress. Rosine. But perhaps he was thinking of marrying her and she was eager to turn this into a kind of dower house so she could get the aunts out of her way. He had evidently tried to impress her with his charm so that he could persuade her to sell the *mas* to him, but Sophie thought that he could prove difficult to interview. His expression was most forbidding when Rosine even touched on the subject of his accident, and if she were to obtain an intimate portrait of the man, she would have to know everything about him, his previous life and the reason why he had given up the glamorous career he had followed and hidden himself away in this little corner of France.

The white shadow of an owl flew low over her head and she saw it descend into a hole in the roof where the tiles had been dislodged. There must be a tremendous lot of work to be done to the house and garden before she could possibly hope to let it to visitors, but she was not to be put off from her plan by Fabien and Rosine.

A silver moon was rising over the snowy blossom of the cherry-trees and, from a thicket close by, a nightingale was singing in cascading fountains of pure melody. The air was warm and sweet as honey with the spicy fragrance of lavender and thyme borne towards her on a gentle breeze. She thought of Fabien and Rosine driving through this azure night, perhaps pausing to make love in some moonlit glade, and she felt restless, depressed and lonely. This, she thought, is ridiculous. Why should the idea of them together make her feel dissatisfied with her own most full and satisfactory life? She was letting herself be carried away by the romantic atmosphere of this place, the moonlight, the fragrant scents and the seductive trills of that small brown bird. As for romance, who needed it? So why should she feel herself to be as sad as the cry of that owl gliding through the silver air like a white-feathered phantom?

CHAPTER TWO

In spite of the unaccustomed noises of the night, the hoot of the owl on the roof, the shrill piercing chorus of crickets outside in the darkness and the monotonous chorus of frogs from the ancient pool, Sophie slept well and woke up feeling refreshed and in a completely different mood, happy and eager to get on as quickly as possible with the renovation of her cottage.

She breakfasted frugally on some black coffee and the remains of the baguette, extremely tough and unrecognisable from the crisp delicious bread of the day before. But dunking it in the fragrant brew in the wide golden pottery bowl made it fractionally more edible and, after she had breakfasted, Sophie felt ready to face going into the village, interviewing the *notaire* and making enquiries concerning possible workmen to help her with her task. She simply must get some help if she was to organise the whole thing in the short time that had been allowed her. Goodness knows when she could come here again for any length of time. In future she would have to fly to Perpignan and hire a car just for the weekend. But if she could obtain workmen to get on with the renovation of the *mas*, she would know that in her absence the place was coming to life again.

She started her little car without trouble and bumped once more along the rough road that led eventually to the village. This was not very large. Straggling roads lined by old grey houses led to a village centre where this morning there were a few market stalls set up under the chestnut trees that were just breaking into bud. Old women in dark printed overalls and black shawls inspected the vegetables carefully before filling their baskets, and frightened-looking hares gazed mournfully out of small hutches, while a few speckled fowls clucked and pecked at their saucers of corn. Sophie took the opportunity to buy salad greens, yellow and red peppers, courgettes and beautiful globe artichokes, olives, fresh eggs and goat's cheese. The women stallholders looked at her curiously and laughed delightedly at her accent that was obviously very strange to them.

Now, she thought, to go and see the *notaire* and ask for some help as regards labour for the *mas*. She could get her other provisions later, bread, wine, and possibly some ham from the *charcuterie*. She did not intend to do much cooking while she was here.

The *notaire*, whom she had met briefly before when she had called for the key, seemed delighted to see her.

'I can give you the names and addresses of a few men who might be able to help you,' he told her. 'I think you will find they'll be glad of work. As you can see, there's not much happening in the village. Of course many of them have small-holdings like yours and grow vegetables and fruit to sell at the markets around here, and there is a certain amount of work obtainable from the château and one or two other large houses in the vicinity, but you shouldn't have any trouble getting a few men to do your work.'

'I was told it would be very expensive.'

'Of course building is not cheap these days, but Aristide left you a certain amount. His pictures were selling well shortly before he died and his wants were small. There should be enough to pay for some of your renovations and if not there must be his other pictures that he left which could be sold.'

'I wanted to ask you about that. You said something to the effect that you hadn't been able to locate them.'

'That's so, but I should think a close inspection of the *mas* would reveal his hiding-place. He must have put them away for safe keeping or left them with some friend. They are bound to come to light sooner or later.'

And with that rather casual supposition, Sophie had to be satisfied. At least M. Dupont had obligingly opened an

account for her at the local bank and she now had some
funds to be going on with. So now to get her labour. She
would have to get the work on the house started without
delay if she were to see some results before she had to return
to England.

As she made her way along the village street, she thought
she had been wise to come here in the morning for she
remembered that in France after twelve, or at the very
latest twelve-thirty, everything stopped for *déjeuner*, the
most important meal of the day, and after that utter quiet
descended on a village like this until late afternoon. But in
the morning all was busy, and so she queued at the baker's
to get a long crispy baguette and indulged herself at the
patisserie by buying one of the pastries known as Little Nuns,
which she knew were delicious and very fattening, choux
pastry with a creamy filling topped with chocolate and
with a large stretch of the imagination resembling small fat
nuns, the dumpy shape of the lower part topped by a small
chocolate-covered head.

The *charcuterie* was equally crowded with women buying
all kinds of cooked meats and quiches and salads of every
kind. It was difficult to resist trying too much of the
delicious-looking food but Sophie, remembering how small
the tiny ice-box was, contented herself with buying some
smoked ham and a small cooked chicken together with
stuffed tomatoes and green peppers stuffed with rice and
herbs and feta cheese.

Tearing herself away from the delights of the small shops
and the interested chatter of the locals, she referred to the
addresses the *notaire* had given her. None of the houses
indicated could be very far away. She expected that she
would find some of the men working in their plots for she
had seen some of them as she drove into the village, figures
bent over spades, dressed in dark trousers and waistcoats
and wearing navy peaked caps or black berets. She drove
therefore to the outskirts of the village where she had seen
the larger vegetable gardens surrounded by wire fences.

Yes, here was one of the places M. Dupont had indicated and this must be the man himself, a rugged individual with large shoulders who was holding his spade as if it had been a toy in his big hands.

Sophie got out of her car and approached the fence.

'M. Jacques?' she called out.

The man stopped his labours, and leaning on his implement looked at her enquiringly.

'*Bonjour*, Mademoiselle. *Que voulez vous?*'

At first he did not seem to understand Sophie's careful high-school French.

'Monsieur, I wish to have some building done, some repairs to my house. M. Dupont gave me your name. Would it be possible to discuss this . . .'

Sophie could not understand why the man's pleasant smile turned to a frown. Had she said something wrong to offend him? But no, he was smiling again but this time shaking his head.

'*Hélas, mademoiselle*, I would have liked to help you but I am starting on another job tomorrow. I have been without work for some time but only this morning I accepted an offer to do some building. I reckon it will take about a month to complete it.'

'Do you know of anyone else who would be willing to help me? I have these names from M. Dupont.'

He took the piece of paper in his grubby hand and Sophie could see he was holding it upside down.

'*Hélas, mademoiselle*, I do not think any of these men are looking for work. You have been misinformed. None of them are in need of work at this moment.'

Sophie was puzzled by his flat denial. Obviously he could not read so how was it that he was so sure none of them would be able to work for her? There was something odd about this. She made up her mind to go to see these men whose addresses the *notaire* had give her in spite of M. Jacques' saying they did not need work.

But as she progressed through the village, she met the

same story. *Quel dommage!* Each one had been in need of work for some time but only this morning they had accepted an offer to do some repairs. She began to think it was too much of a coincidence that all her potential builders should have been snatched away from her. When she had heard the same story from the seventh man, she began to feel there was something very odd about the whole thing, but try as she might, she could not get from any of them where they were going to start work the very next day. They pretended they did not understand her French, although they had understood it perfectly well when she had asked if they could work for her.

I expect they think it's none of my business, she thought. But what bad luck that they had all been spoken for! She even tried to ask the crowd of men who had come to the village square now the morning market had packed up and were starting to play *boule*, but these gnarled veterans were inclined to laugh at her. Couldn't she see for herself that their working days were over?

By twelve she had got no further and everyone in the village seemed to be heading homewards for lunch, the long baguettes thrust under their arms. Completely frustrated, she headed back to her car, for if she was to have *déjeuner* at the château, she would have to hurry. It was only her first day here, she told herself, but she had hoped to get the building going straight away. Surely there must be someone in the village who hadn't been offered some building job that was starting tomorrow? Maybe she could ask for advice at the château, but she hesitated at begging favours from Fabien.

She supposed she had better change into something more respectable than denim jeans if she was to lunch with Fabien's two old aunts. From the scanty wardrobe she had brought with her she chose a dress of lavender cotton sprigged with small white flowers, something utterly different from her usual working-girl outfit of chic Chanel-type suit and high-necked blouse. She repaired her make-up, the powder luminous over her matt ivory skin and her lipstick a shade of rose that did not clash with the shining copper of her hair.

The château was not far away. Fabien was right when he said he was her nearest neighbour. It was simple to find the track through the woodland until she came to a wide, impressive gate of intricately worked wrought iron, flanked by two stone columns on the top of which were two fierce sculptured lions rampant. The gates had been left open so she drove through and, leaving the grassy track behind, she found herself on a well-kept driveway, lined by upright poplar trees.

As she rounded a bend the château came into view, a fairy-tale mansion with turrets at each side built of silver-grey stone. The gardens were very formal, geometric beds of flowers in shades of pink, blue and yellow edged with clipped borders of lavender and box. There were orange-trees in tubs placed symmetrically at the corners of the neat beds and there were still some oranges from last season glowing like jewels against dark leaves. Why should he want to buy her little cottage, Sophie thought, when he has all this?

The old bell-pull echoed eerily from somewhere inside the château and, as Sophie stood there, a silky-coated golden spaniel sidled up to her from its seat in the sunny garden and pushed against her, waiting hopefully for the door to be opened. An elderly maid came to the door. She looked, thought Sophie, as if she had been there for ever, the old-fashioned kind of *bonne*, in black dress and apron and with grey hair sleeked down from a middle parting.

There was a hallway with curving double staircase and Sophie got a fleeting impression of oriental rugs in jewel colours and dark family portraits on the walls before she was shown into the salon. Here, in contrast to the rather dark entrance hall, Sophie had an impression of lightness and grace. A pale blue Aubusson carpet garlanded with yellow wreaths of roses covered most of the shining wood floor and high windows were festooned with gold silk curtains from floor to ceiling, looped back with cabled ropes of gold braid. Delicate gilded chairs and sofas were upholstered in pastel colours of pink, green, yellow and turquoise and there were several very elaborate pieces of furniture in beautiful woods with intricate inlaid patterns and gilded decorations.

A log fire burned in the delicately wrought silver grate below the graceful lines of the carved mantel and, in upright chairs on either side, sat two old ladies whom on first sight Sophie took for twins, for they were dressed in seemingly identical outfits, black silk ankle-length dresses, cobweb shawls of white wool, silver-buckled shoes, white lace caps upon their silver curls and, as they rose to welcome her, she saw that they were both leaning upon ebony canes with silver handles.

But almost immediately she realised that perhaps her first impression of complete similarity had been wrong. There was a great difference between them. The old lady on the right was definitely the leader.

'Ah, the *petite* Sophie, niece of our good friend Aristide, *enchantée de vous voir*,' she declared in a strong, ringing voice.

'It is most kind of you to have me here,' said Sophie.

'Not at all. I am Germaine and this is Isabelle.'

Sophie turned to greet the other old lady and now she realised that, in spite of their resemblance to each other, they were two completely different types. Germaine had strong features and in them one could trace a likeness to Fabien, with the aristocratic nose and chin like something on an old cameo. The dark eyes were bright and highly intelligent and the hands that held the silver-knobbed stick were the colour of old ivory as was the almost unwrinkled face above the high lace collar.

Isabelle on the other hand gave the impression of a faded rose, her delicately pink face wrinkled into small criss-cross lines, her small chin receding into a collar that was more frilly than her sister's. Her eyes looked vague but her nose still had something of a retroussé charm. There were more frills and tucks on the dark silk of her dress, whereas Germaine's had a style and cut which, though old-fashioned, spoke of the simplicity of Paris.

Unlike Germaine, Isabelle spoke in a faint, soft voice. 'My dear Sophie, I am so glad to meet any relative of our dear Aristide. *Regardes*, Germaine, she has the same colour of hair as he had.'

'But she is a very little more beautiful, *n'est-ce pas*, Tante Belle?'

Fabien had come quietly into the room and with his coming it seemed to Sophie as if the whole atmosphere changed. His vibrant masculinity seemed to overwhelm the ambience of lavender and lace and delicate beautiful furniture. But it was obvious the two aunts adored him, even if Germaine's expression was more restrained than Isabelle's.

Isabelle seemed to have taken his joking remark very seriously, for she came up to Sophie and, producing some silver lorgnettes, peered at her with faded blue eyes that must once have been very pretty.

'Yes, you are right, Fabien. She is lovely, but what would you expect from a niece of Aristide's? He was always very handsome. Why did you never come to visit him, my dear?'

'I wish I had known him but I hardly knew he existed until I had his bequest. He was a great-uncle, of course, and somehow the family had lost touch with him.'

'*Dommage*. A pity. He was a great man and a wonderful lover.'

Germaine rapped on the kerb of the fireplace with her stick. She looked, thought Sophie, as if she would willingly have used it upon some person.

'*Tais-toi*, Belle. Sophie is not interested in Aristide's love-life. Such things should be forgotten when the man, we hope, is in Paradise.'

'And if he is not yet there, he soon will be, for I pray for him every day,' said Isabelle.

'We know you do, Tante Belle, so don't worry any more about it,' said Fabien very gently and soothingly. 'Now let me give you all some of our own aperitif. I think you will like it, Sophie. It was made in a good year of our *vendage*, our grape harvest.'

He poured a measure of wine into a clear crystal glass where it glowed with the colour of rubies, then motioned her to come and sit beside him in the deep embrasure of a window-seat looking out over the green lawns and the terrace where peacocks strutted with iridescent tails sweeping the ancient stone. She hesitated, wondering whether the old aunts would like this or whether they would expect her to sit nearer to them, but they nodded approvingly so there was nothing else for it but to take her place near to him and face the quizzical expression of those dark eyes.

'*Vous avez bien dormi?*' he asked her. 'But I need not ask that. I can see you slept well even if you were in strange surroundings. Not a hint of a shadow under those so beautiful blue eyes. And the intruder did not show himself, no?'

'No,' Sophie asserted firmly. 'Could be that intruder was just a figment of someone's imagination, an excuse for coming to look over the property.'

He need not think he could win her over with his flattery, Sophie thought, for yesterday he had given her a terrible fright and later he had shocked her by the news that he was thinking he might buy the *mas*. He needed to be put in his place. And his place was here in this elegant château, not in her delightful, shabby little cottage.

The teasing smile died on his lips and the haughty profile turned away from her looked very different from the laughing man of a moment ago.

'I need no excuse, *mademoiselle*, to look at property that is within my boundary, but there was indeed a report of someone living there. Do you think I would lie to you?'

'Yes, I do,' Sophie stated. 'I don't think you would have

any such scruples if it suited your purpose.'

Rather to her surprise, he flung back his head and laughed heartily. The old aunts, startled by the noise, smiled appreciatively at Sophie as if they approved the fact that Fabien seemed to be enjoying her company.

'*Quel horreur!* What an impression you seem to have gained of me from one short evening's acquaintance. I will have to do better in future, I can see.'

'But according to you, there is to be no future for me here, or so I understood from your friend Rosine last night.'

'We'll talk about that later,' said Fabien, smiling again with all his former charm. 'Here comes Bernadette to announce that *déjeuner* is served.'

The walls of the dining-room were panelled and hung with family portraits, some of which bore a striking resemblance to Fabien. There was a vast circular table of some light brown wood, the grain of which had been worked so that it showed an exquisite design similar to the tail feathers of an ostrich. At each place lace mats were surrounded by heavy silver in an elaborate design, and in the centre was a silver epergne held by winged cupids and holding an arrangement of jasmine and white freesias with trailing green fern.

The meal was light and beautifully cooked, chicken *bouillon*, sole cooked in a creamy sauce with shrimps and mushrooms, *compôte* of fruit in delicate baskets made of biscuit. It was accompanied by a white wine that seemed to Sophie, carried away by the beauty of her surroundings, to have the very fragrance of spring.

'Oh, yes, we are not idle here,' Fabien assured her. 'We have a flourishing wine business from the château. You should have come in September when we have the *vendage*.'

'How Aristide loved our *vendage*,' Isabelle murmured. 'You must have seen some of his pictures he painted in the vineyards and caves, the cellars where the wine is made.'

'No, I have not. As a matter of fact I have not seen any of Aristide's paintings,' Sophie told her.

'Fabien has one or two hanging in his office at the cave,' Germaine informed her. 'They are hardly suitable for a salon, we thought. A little too avant-garde, but I understand they are very popular now. What is it, Belle?'

Isabelle, or Belle as they seemed to call her, was giggling like a schoolgirl. She put her hands up to her face.

'Pardon. I was just thinking, Germaine, how droll it would have been if Papa had ever seen the portraits dear Aristide did of me when we were young.'

Germaine rose from the table and took Belle by the hand.

'Time for our siesta, Belle. Fabien will look after our guest. It has been delightful to meet you, Sophie. We'll look forward to seeing you many times while you are staying here.'

'I don't expect she will be staying long, Germaine,' said Belle. 'She is going to sell the house to Fabien, *n'est-ce pas?*'

'It is not yet decided, Belle. Now come.'

'Oh, but surely Fabien has decided and he always gets what he desires, just like Papa. Fabien is headstrong just like all the de Cressacs, but Rosine may know how to make him happy. I know all about such things because I too knew how to keep Aristide content.'

She smiled at Sophie with her vague blue eyes but seemed to be seeing some scene from a long time ago.

'*Au revoir*, Sophie. I am glad you look like Aristide. You could have been his daughter. His daughter and mine. If only Papa had been more understanding.'

Germaine seemed to hustle her out of the room before she could say any more.

'If you have finished your coffee, we could take a turn in the grounds,' Fabien suggested.

They did not go into the formal garden at the front of the château but into a place where sweeping lawns led to a lake with woodlands around. It was very quiet here under the trees. Even the birds seemed to be taking their siesta and only an occasional rustling in the leaves or a drowsy note betrayed them. There were cherry-trees too, sprinkling a carpet of white petals over the pathway, filling the air with their sweet almondy scent.

'They have been allowed to run wild here,' Fabien told her. 'We no longer harvest cherries, only grapes for our wines. You should have come at the time of the *vendage*. It's all go then.'

'That's a long time away,' Sophie said. 'Maybe I'll manage that too when I have got the *mas* in order.'

She stumbled over some hidden stone in the path and he straight away put his arm around her to hold her steady. His hand was firm and strong through the thin fabric of her dress.

'There, you are safe now,' he told her.

But she did not feel safe. This close contact was too intimate when all she wanted was to go on feeling indignant at the aunts' clear assumption that he would get his own way and be able to buy the *mas* with no denial on her part.

'You will have gathered from the conversation at lunchtime that Belle had some kind of affair with Aristide, or at least she thinks she had. Poor Belle. She lives in the past a lot now. A great mistake for anyone, don't you think? One should never look back.'

She was conscious of his hand now, holding her shoulder in a bruising grip. He seemed to have forgotten she was there. She thought this too-firm hold was somehow an expression of his inner mind. He would have held the branch of a tree just as strongly.

'Sometimes it's good to look back,' she demurred. 'Surely all memories can't be bad.'

'Perhaps not, but it is sentimental to look back. Once a thing has happened there is little to be done by remembering. The only thing to do is to cultivate the art of forgetting. Not always easy, but it can be done if one has enough determination.'

So that's how he feels about his past, thought Sophie. His bitter tone contrasted very strongly with the previous lighthearted, almost flirtatious manner he had previously shown to her. It was not going to be easy to find out about his previous career, and that was what interested her editor. She thought she must try to recall their conversations. It might all come in useful later. How she wished she could use a tape recorder, but of course that was impossible. She must try to rely on her good memory and jot down her impressions later.

'You make it sound as if you have things from your past life that hurt you to think about,' she suggested tentatively.

She thought, if only she could get him to talk to her about it, she could succeed in getting the intimate profile her editor needed. But it was early days yet and she had been incredibly fortunate to make his acquaintance so soon.

He laughed scornfully.

'You know very little about me, Mademoiselle Sophie, if you think I could allow anything out of the past to hurt me. At one time in my life I lived in the glare of publicity. I learned then to develop the hide of a rhinoceros when it came to taking notice of anything that was said against me.'

'That's interesting,' said Sophie innocently. 'May I ask what was the cause of this publicity?'

'You may ask but I won't necessarily tell you. Let's say I was a little wild in my youth and led the kind of life that seems to be of interest to these so-called gentlemen of the press. If there's one thing I can't stand, it's the profession, if you can call it that, of journalism. All journalists are anathema to me. I hate the whole tribe. They are no better than a pack of jackals, worse in fact, for, in the wild, jackals serve a useful purpose in scavenging, cleaning up debris the lions have left.'

'Couldn't journalists be doing something like that too?' Sophie suggested. 'Bringing to public view important subjects that otherwise would pass unnoticed? Surely sometimes they do that kind of public service?'

He shook his head, his expression dark and frowning.

'I can do without that kind of cleaning up. Rather say

that they love to stir things up that are best forgotten. No, I hate journalists who try to expose one's innermost soul to the world's view. Since I chose to live a private life, I have no longer been worried by them, *grâce à Dieu.* But let's choose a more interesting subject for our conversation, Sophie. Let's talk about you. You surely can't be serious when you say you intend to go to all the trouble of rebuilding the *mas?*'

'I am indeed,' declared Sophie. 'If only I can find someone to help me,' she added rather wistfully. 'For some odd reason the villagers that the *notaire* recommended to me are all occupied with someone else's buildings.'

'Ah yes, but I think I warned you it would be difficult to find people.'

'You said it would be expensive.'

'That too. Now, Sophie, let's talk business. I need the *mas* for my own use. It is on my ground and should be part of the estate of the château. It was only because Aristide was so friendly with my father, the old *Comte*, that the arrangement was made. Now I'm willing to buy it back for three times the sum that Aristide paid. Isn't that generous for a broken-down building? With the amount I'm willing to pay you you could easily buy a place on the coast, a place which would be much more suitable for you and your friends to spend your vacations.'

'But I don't want a house on the coast,' Sophie protested. 'I want it here. Don't you understand, I'm in love with the idea of living in this part of France, right off the tourist area. If I want to go to the sea, I can get there quite easily from here. I don't have to live there with all the other tourists.'

He had dropped his hand from her shoulder and they were standing facing each other. The slumbrous heat of the afternoon seemed to wrap the woods in silence. It was the kind of day to be lying with a lover in cool green shade but here she was, thought Sophie, intensely angry with this man who seemed to want to push aside all her dreams for his own selfish ends.

'How can you say you are in love with this part of France?' he sneered. 'You only arrived here yesterday and you don't know anything of the country. I dare say you know nothing of building either, so how can you hope with your schoolgirl French to cope with workmen whose preferred language could be Catalan anyway?'

'I know I could do it,' Sophie declared. 'I know more about this part of the country than you think. I've studied all the books I could lay hands on that would tell me about it.'

'Books! Probably journalists' impressions after a month-long holiday. Take it from me, you would be much happier if you accepted my offer and bought yourself a house on the coast. If you must live in this area, the Côte Vermeille offers houses that are completely suitable for your purpose. That way you would be saved all the hassle of trying to make something out of that old ruin.'

'I want the hassle, as you call it,' cried Sophie indignantly. 'It was all to be part of the fun of having inherited it. Can't you realise it was wonderful to hear I had inherited the *mas*? Before that Aristide had always seemed something of a legend in our family. I had heard so much about him and I'd always wanted to come here but somehow it never happened. Now I'm here and I'm quite sure he didn't intend that I should sell the place and buy a house on the coast. If he'd wanted me to do that he would have said so. What he did say was that he hoped I would get as much happiness from the *mas* as he had always had. So I don't intend to sell it, however persuasive you try to be.'

'We'll see about that,' sneered Fabien. 'If it's the amount of money you would have to pay for a house on the coast that's worrying you, I can always meet you on that.'

Sophie had a primitive urge to hit the confident smile from that handsome brown face. At the same time she wanted to stamp and scream at him.

'You really are incorrigible. Haven't I got through to

you at all? I'm trying to tell you I love the *mas*. Even if I have to live in it just as it is, I'll do it. Even if I have to do the renovations myself, I'll learn how to lay bricks. I'm determined that I won't give it up. Don't you understand I want a house that is old and has a history and has been lived in? I don't want some smart box of a villa that was put up last year and is just like a hundred others on the coast.'

'Just like a woman. You have some romantic dream of renovating the place. But what do you know about how a Catalan *mas* should look? No, if I know how the English think southern houses should be, you will probably paint it pink.'

'I most certainly will not.'

'And as for your dislike of the houses at the coast, you have not seen them yet. Suppose I take you out for the day tomorrow and we'll have a look at a possible choice.'

He was like a juggernaut, thought Sophie, rolling aside all her plans. Or trying to. But just because he was used to getting his own way, it didn't say that was going to work with her. On the other hand, if she said she would go to the coast with him tomorrow, it would mean she would be spending the whole day in his company and it might suit her purpose. If she was very cunning, and led the conversation that way, she might lead him to tell her more about himself.

'If you insist, I'll go to the coast with you, but I promise nothing. I'm determined to do up the *mas*. If only the workmen were not all occupied. I just hate whoever has given them employment just as I needed them.'

'Good. I'll look forward to that. I'm sure you may change your mind once you have seen how beautiful the coastline is not so very far away from here. I'll call for you fairly early. This is not a busy time in the vineyards and the other work of the château can be done by my supervisor.'

Now he had got her consent to his plan, he seemed to become more relaxed, but she herself still felt shaken by his determination to have the *mas*. But it was ridiculous to feel so upset. She only had to keep giving him a firm no to all his persuasions, and tomorrow or the next day surely she could find someone who would be willing to work for her. Meanwhile she must do her best to keep friendly with him however impossible he seemed to her, for she was still just as keen to get this profile published, even more keen now she realised how complicated he seemed. That was just the kind of human-interest story that her editor would appreciate.

Fabien had so far drawn a veil over his past, but that made her all the more eager to succeed in finding out what had happened to make him turn his back on society. It was all very well for him to dismiss the past as if it had never happened, but that tragedy on the mountain seemed to have completely changed his way of life and she was determined to get the full story.

Strolling back, they had left the woodlands by another path and found themselves in the courtyard at the back of the château, a place where there were stables and garages and where quite a lot of different kinds of work seemed to be going on. A truck had just come in by the wide gateway and the driver descended and instantly engaged another man in animated conversation. As they approached, the one man came up to Fabien.

'*Pardon, M. le Comte*, but the building materials have come. Shall I send a message to the village to tell the men we engaged that they can come tomorrow for certain? Everything is ready to start work. With the extra help you managed today, we should be able to finish the repairs in about one month. That old ruin of a summer-house has been like that since the old *Comte's* time. It's been badly neglected for years. However, the men are pleased now that you have made such an urgent job of it.'

'Certainly, Jean-Paul, you can start on the work tomorrow. You have my instructions. I myself will be away for the day but I know I can trust you to get it all going.'

Sophie waited until they were clear of the courtyard and

standing near her little car before she could bring herself to speak.

'So it was you!' she declared. 'You were this mysterious employer who had suddenly given work to men who had been without work for months.'

Fabien remained completely unperturbed. His dark eyes regarded her with a level gaze and he did not seem in the least embarrassed by her discovery.

'Certainly. There is what the English, I believe, call a folly, a kind of ancient summer-house in the grounds that I have been intending to renovate for a long time. Now with summer approaching it seems the ideal time to get on with it. It will be a charming place where the aunts can sit in the sun, or out of it as they wish, and enjoy the views of the garden while doing their needlework or entertaining their friends. I myself hope to enjoy it too. Who knows, perhaps it will be finished before you go and you can see what a charming place it is going to be.'

'And when did you decide on this plan?' Sophie asked coldly.

'*N'importe*. What does it matter? I have been intending to do something about it for a long time, but yesterday Rosine reminded me of it. She thinks it will be a wonderful idea to have it ready for the hot months of summer.'

'Very clever of her,' said Sophie bitterly. 'And meanwhile you have taken all the available workmen from the village, just at the time when I need them.'

Fabien flung his hands wide and treated her to his most charming smile.

'Ah, Sophie, do not be cross, I beg you. You cannot be serious about rebuilding the *mas*. When I have shown you our coastline, you will fall in love with it, just as you say you have fallen in love with the *mas*, but think how much trouble you will be saved. You will want to accept my offer without any doubt.'

'If you think that, you don't know me very well, but I feel I'm getting to know a lot about you, and what I know I dislike heartily,' Sophie declared. 'I think it's most despicable that you did this thing to me, when I had told you how desperately I wanted to rebuild the *mas*. I said I could hate the person who took all the builders and it's quite true. I was so pleased when I came here, so glad to have the *mas*, and I didn't realise that there would be an arrogant man here who, because he has always had his own way, would block me at every turn.'

She felt she would have liked to do some damage to that handsome, smiling face. He looked completely unperturbed by her outburst and she felt at a distinct disadvantage because she was trembling with anger.

'Come, come, Sophie, I am not such a wicked person as all that. Don't derange yourself. Tomorrow when I show you the coast, you will change your mind and be convinced that my ideas are completely right.'

'Will I indeed?' Sophie demanded. 'I suppose it would never occur to you that you could be mistaken. I don't want to go with you to your wretched coast but now I suppose I'll have to just to prove you wrong.'

Much to her surprise, Fabien took her hand and kissed it. Looking down on the dark shining wing of his head, she felt the rough male touch of his chin upon the smooth back of her hand. It gave her an odd sensation of intimacy and she snatched her hand away.

'You will come, Sophie, not because you have to but because we will have a pleasant day, I promise you that. So no more fighting. By tomorrow evening I think you will have changed your mind on quite a few things including your very bad opinion of me.'

Never, thought Sophie, as she drove away from the château to her more humble dwelling place. She was amazed at his arrogance. How could he have been so blatantly horrible as to block completely any hope she had of rebuilding her inheritance?

CHAPTER THREE

ONCE back at the *mas*, Sophie had spent the rest of the afternoon slashing away at the waist-high weeds, trying to make some kind of impression on the part of the garden that was immediately in front of the house. Although it didn't seem to be a great deal of use, she felt she must make a start at clearing the place. What she really needed was some technical advice on how to set about repairing the building.

As she waged war on the wild vegetation with a scythe that she had found in an outhouse, she thought about Fabien and seemed to be working out her aggressive feeling towards him as she hit out at the thistles and the dock. Why had she consented to waste a whole day of her precious leave in going on what must only prove a fruitless journey to the coast? She had no intention of selling the *mas* to him and purchasing a seaside villa, however persuasive he might be.

But then there was the question of finding out enough about that past life of his to write the article required by Mike. In a way she wished she had never embarked on this. Feeling as she did at the moment, she did not want to know any more about the man. To write a profile of someone, one must have a certain sympathy with him, and now she felt she had none at all. She was not even interested to find out more about him. She felt she knew too much already.

Although by lighting a fire under the tank she had managed a hot shower before she went to bed, she woke up feeling distinctly stiff from the unaccustomed labour. It was all very well to vow that she would do it herself if all else failed, but she was not used to manual work and the very thought of Fabien surrounded by all those workmen made her feel very angry indeed.

Today denim jeans would not do, she thought, and she put on a dress in a shade of mimosa yellow that had shoestring straps under the short matching jacket that was piped with white. Her legs had already become golden from all her exposure to the sun yesterday and she wore a pair of strappy white and yellow sandals that matched her outfit. Splashing a flowery cologne on her arms and breast, she thought that she must really invest in some of the canvas espadrilles that seemed to be the accepted footwear in this part of the country.

Drinking her coffee from the yellow pottery bowl, she thought she had had enough of stale baguette yesterday so today she ate oatcakes from a tin she had brought with her. There seemed to be no solution to the problem of getting fresh bread here unless she went to fetch it each morning from the *boulangerie*. If only she had been able to employ someone from the village, she could have asked him to bring her fresh bread, but that was the least of her troubles.

She was startled to hear the phone ringing in the living-room from its place on an old oak desk. The *notaire* had told her he had had it reinstalled for her benefit but she had not expected to get a message so soon. Lifting the receiver, she was just trying to murmur some appropriate phrase in French, when her editor's voice came over the wires loud and clear.

'Hi, there, Sophie. You've arrived safely?'

'Yes, Mike, I'm here. But how did you know where to find me?'

'You left the number on your desk. Now tell me, Sophie, how's the assignment going?'

'Good grief, Mike, give me a chance. I only arrived two days ago.'

'Time enough, Sophie. Have you met him yet?'

'Yes, I have, unfortunately.'

'Why do you say that?'

'He's the most arrogant man I've ever met. I'm sorry I ever said I'd do this for you.'

'Sounds interesting. I know you'll make a good job of it, Sophie. If anyone can get a story out of even the most unpromising subject, it's you. There's a new expedition planned on the Eiger and this will all tie in so I want it as quickly as you can do it.'

'I thought this was supposed to be my vacation, Mike.'

'Oh, I know you'll be able to manage both. How is the *mas* by the way?'

'In ruins, and your wonderful Fabien de Cressac has just employed all the available labour for some work of his own just to spite me because he wants to buy the *mas*.'

Completely ignoring her complaints, she heard Mike say, 'That's great, Sophie, it sounds as if you have become really friendly with him.'

'Friendly,' exclaimed Sophie. 'I can't stand him. He's taking me to the coast today to try to sell me the idea of buying a house there.'

'That's my girl. Don't worry too much about the *mas*. Keep your eye on the main object. If you do well with this article, who knows, maybe there will be a little promotion in sight. And don't forget I want photographs too. He's a handsome devil from what I remember.'

'Too handsome for his own good,' cried Sophie.

'It all sounds great. I'm expecting something really smashing from you this time, Sophie. I know you won't let me down. Bye now.'

She was left staring at the receiver. It was no use trying to explain anything to Mike. He had a one-track mind when it came to getting anything newsworthy and it seemed she was committed now to writing this article. But after Fabien's tirade yesterday on the subject of journalists, she had better take care not to reveal her profession to him. What if he asked her about her work? She could say she had a secretarial job, which was partly true for she certainly did enough typing. But possibly he would not even ask. He was only interested in selling her the idea of buying a villa by the coast. He was not interested in her as a person and she must remember that if he tried to be charming to her, as he probably would. She remembered the old aunts saying that Fabien always got his own way. Well, this time he's going to be frustrated, she vowed to herself.

He arrived in a very streamlined sports-car of gleaming silver with red leather upholstery and an open top.

'You had better have a scarf for your head. Rosine always ties her hair up when she comes with me,' Fabien advised, but Sophie thought it seemed such a calm sunny day that she would risk having the wind in her hair, and as they picked up speed on the main road, glancing at her, Fabien said, 'You look like a Norse goddess going into battle with that shining red-gold hair streaming behind you, but you, Sophie, deal out the sharp edge of your tongue rather than your sword, don't you?'

'Only if I'm provoked, Fabien,' Sophie replied. 'I'm usually the most peaceful of women.'

'What? With that copper-coloured hair? I can't believe it.'

They were driving through sun-baked rolling country, the colour of gold. On all the slopes there were waves of vineyards, small gnarled branches just sprouting the spring covering of light green that would be transformed in the autumn to leafy vines bearing plump bunches of grapes. It was not long before a blue line of ocean appeared on the horizon and soon they were descending in long sweeping curves of the road to the cluster of tiled roofs, white, blue and rosy red, where the town of Collioure clung to the curve of the bay, an inlet of the blue Mediterranean sea.

'Why, it's lovely here,' Sophie could not help exclaiming, forgetting that she had been determined not to show any enthusiasm.

'I knew you would like it,' Fabien told her, looking very

satisfied with her reaction.

He found a place above the harbour to park the car and they strolled down towards the beach through the narrow streets. Being early in the season, it was not particularly crowded and in the alleys cats were sitting stretched out to full length enjoying the balmy warmth of the sun that had not yet reached summer heat. There were fascinating little shops, their windows filled with holiday souvenirs, and Sophie was particularly attracted to the bright table-linen in woven patterns that Fabien informed her were typical of Catalan design.

'Collioure is known as an artists' paradise,' Fabien told her. 'It's possible we may be able to find some of Aristide's work in the galleries here.'

'Do you mean there might be some still on sale here?'

'No, I don't mean that. They would be privately owned, possibly lent to galleries or bought by them when Aristide was alive. Of late his paintings have always been snapped up as soon as he offered them for sale. They had become very fashionable.'

'He is supposed to have left some to me but so far there is no trace of them.'

'That seems odd, but, knowing Aristide, I'd say that towards the end of his life he may have been a little confused. He may have thought he had pictures to leave but forgotten that he had already sold them. But what does it matter? If he did sell them, the money must be in the bank for you.'

'Perhaps,' said Sophie. 'But it is rather strange that he specially mentioned these pictures in his will. They were early ones that he valued highly and had never wanted to sell.'

Sophie seemed to detect a withdrawn expression on Fabien's face that she did not know how to interpret. But perhaps she was imagining it. Was he bored with her talk of Aristide's lost paintings? Did he think she was making a fuss about something that possibly had this simple explanation, the one he had offered, that Aristide had sold them and forgotten the fact?

'I should very much like to see some of his paintings if there are some in the studios here,' she said now.

'I think they are paintings of Collioure done in his own particular style. They are unlike his earlier work. I believe at first he excelled at portraits, but these are some that I think he did probably for his own amusement.'

She could well believe this when she saw one in the small exclusive gallery to which he took her. By this time she had realised what he meant when he said that Collioure was an artists' paradise, for at every turning and all along the sea-front there were people painting their versions of the scenery, the beach, the cathedral in the curve of the bay, the narrow streets. If they were not painting, they were standing beside a collection of pictures hoping to sell them to the tourists. There were good paintings and bad paintings of the same scenes, but when Sophie saw the one Aristide had painted, she realised that here was something completely different. It was what she believed could be called an example of primitive painting. There was Collioure with its beach and the turrets behind it, but upon the beach was a highly coloured fishing boat and a huge fish almost like a whale grounded with a collection of people in bright clothes all looking at it in wonder.

'It's most attractive,' she said. 'I could wish it were mine.'

'Alas, *mademoiselle*, it is not for sale,' said the bearded assistant. 'Unfortunately it is the only example of M. Aristide's work that we have been able to procure. Since his death they have increased in value. I wish I had been able to get more of his work.'

'Would you be interested in getting more if I were able to offer you any?' asked Sophie.

'Indeed, yes, but do you mean to say, *mademoiselle*, that you know some source of supply?'

'I might,' Sophie told him.

'Mademoiselle is the niece of M. Aristide,' Fabien explained. 'He is supposed to have left her the remnant of his work, but they have not come to light yet. Personally I don't think they will. I'm sure he must have sold them already and forgotten about it.'

'How can you be so sure?' cried Sophie. 'He specially mentioned them in his will. He said he was leaving them to me as well as the *mas*.'

'A will that was made some months before he died. He probably sold them and forgot he had ever intended you should have them.'

Sophie wondered why Fabien should be so dampening about Aristide's pictures. She herself, now she had seen an example of his work, was very keen to find them. Even if she had to sell some of them to pay for the repairs to the *mas*, she might still be able to keep one or two.

'If you do find them, please, *mademoiselle*, I beg you to give me first refusal,' the owner of the gallery implored her.

So now she knew where she could sell the pictures if ever they came to light. She must conduct a search as soon as possible, for she was convinced that Aristide had intended her to have them. He had even mentioned in his will that he hoped they would help her if she wished to renovate the *mas*.

Everything about the little town of Collioure seemed to Sophie to be enchanting and yet she must not show too much enthusiasm because she didn't want Fabien to think he was making his point. However attractive the villas at the coast might be, she was not to be moved from her original purpose to renovate her own little bit of French property, the precious one that Aristide had left especially to her.

They sat at a table on the *plage*, and the sun was hot enough to make them appreciate the umbrella shading the table which was right beside the pebbled curve of the beach surrounding the brilliant blue of the bay. Beside them bronzed men and golden girls in the briefest of swimsuits were sipping long iced drinks or more exotic concoctions in bright pinks and greens in goblets decorated with slices of orange and lemon and tiny parasols which speared cherries and olives. Sophie said she would prefer a tisane made of vervaine and menthe and she drank this while Fabien had a long glass of lager.

She could not help noticing that the alluring women at the tables close to them seemed for the moment to lose interest in their companions and have eyes only for Fabien. He was that kind of man, she decided, the kind who would have an instant appeal for women. But he seemed oblivious of this. He did not even look at them for he seemed to have eyes only for her. His dark glance seemed to take in her whole appearance: first it was on the copper strands of her hair, then on to the shining gleam of her bare shoulders in the yellow sun-dress, a brief look at the place where its low cut showed the gentle division of her breasts, and then back again to her face, the curve of her mouth; finally the penetrating stare seemed to hold her own eyes captive to his own.

She wondered what he could be thinking, but all he said was, 'In spite of that copper hair, I notice you seem to become a delicious shade of gold quite easily, Sophie, and your eyes look even more azure, if that is possible.'

Sophie sighed. If only she could take the scene as it appeared and enjoy sitting in these delightful surroundings with a man of infinite charm. To other women, she hastily added to herself. But she knew that he was using that magnetic glance in order to charm her into saying she would sell the *mas* to him.

'Flattery will get you nowhere, *M. le Comte*,' she told him. 'This is certainly a beautiful, intriguing place, but I am still in love with the *mas*.'

'You have hardly seen anything of it yet,' he told her.

'Come, you shall see the church and the walk beside the sea.'

Out of the brilliant sunshine they came into the impressive seventeenth-century church. To Sophie it seemed such a contrast to the vivid beach life that was going on all around just a few yards from this ancient building that had been built on the rocks as a safe haven to the seafaring people who had inhabited this place long before it became a fashionable resort.

Coming in from the dazzling outside light, into the cool darkness, she stumbled and felt Fabien's arm around her, his hand warm and strong on the bareness of her shoulders. She let it remain there as they wandered in silence up to the splendid golden altar that portrayed Christ in Majesty in baroque style filling the whole wall. After the noisy life of the beach, it seemed such an astonishing change to be here alone with Fabien, the only sounds their footsteps echoing on the stone pavement and, from far above in the roof, the sounds of doves in gentle contrast to the harsh calling of the seagulls outside flying over the water.

'It seems a very peaceful place,' she said.

'At this moment, yes,' he replied, his hand tightening on her shoulder as if he were in the grip of some powerful emotion. 'But in spite of all the prayers that ascended to heaven from this place, seamen were still drowned and ships dashed on the rocks below. When Fate takes a hand, prayers are of little avail, or so I have found.'

'You sound very cynical. Do you speak from experience?' Maybe I can get him to talk now, she thought. He is thinking of that time on the mountain.

'Certainly, but it's a long story and not very interesting to anyone but myself. Come, Sophie. Let's take ourselves out into the sunshine again. You may find this place peaceful, but personally I think it is far too gloomy in spite of all its rich decorations.

'And now to go to an *agence immobilière*,' Fabien announced when they had come out of the church.

'I'm not with you,' Sophie told him, dazzled by the strong sunlight, and trying to take in the view of the glittering sea and panorama of sunlit buildings. 'My French isn't up to that. What does it mean?'

'What you would call an estate agent, I believe. Wouldn't you like to find out what is offered in this place that seems to have enchanted you?'

'Oh, no, you don't,' said Sophie warily. 'I don't want to visit an estate agent. I'd much rather take a walk along that cliff path. There looks an interesting beach further on.'

'Come, Sophie,' Fabien said severely, as if he were talking to a child, thought Sophie indignantly. 'If we don't go now they will be closed and then all the purpose of our visit will be lost.'

'You mean your purpose, not mine,' declared Sophie. 'I told you all along I had no intention of looking at houses here. You can visit the agent if you wish but I mean to explore the cliff path.'

And with that she strode swiftly away from him in the direction of the precipitous path that had been hacked out between the rocks that fell away to the sea, and the cliffs that towered overhead.

'Come back, Sophie,' she heard him cry. 'You must take that path slowly. Don't be so rash.'

But she strode on, almost running now, for she felt furious that he was determined to turn what could have been a pleasant day into a trial of wills. She was certainly not going to be persuaded into going to look at houses she had no intention of buying. She could hear him calling to her and she quickened her step although by now she realised that the path was very narrow and that her sandals were unsuitable for the rough stone. There was no one else about, for it was coming near to noon when all the French ideas turned to having an aperitif preparatory to partaking of *le déjeuner*.

She had come suddenly to a place where a small narrow

bridge swung abruptly over a gulley between the cliffs and she realised all at once that she was going too quickly to negotiate it, but at the same time, she could hear his footsteps pounding away some distance behind her. She tried to swing around to face him and with that she lost her balance and felt herself falling through the ropes that were placed there to guard passers-by. Desperately her hands went out and she managed to grasp on to the edge of the bridge as it swayed above her with the impetus of her fall, and there she was hanging over a drop of some thirty feet with water and rocks below. Her arms felt as if they were being jerked out of their sockets and she felt her hands slipping on the rough wood of the bridge.

And then he was there, kneeling above her, and she realised with a shock that his face that normally looked the colour of golden oak was pallid and grey.

'Can you hold on for a moment?' he asked her, almost in a whisper. 'I must stretch my arms to get you by the shoulders in order to support your weight.'

For a long moment it seemed to Sophie as if he would not be able to get to her before her hands gave way under the strain, but now she felt his hands supporting her and it was such a blessed relief that she felt tears rain down her face. His hands were like iron paining the softness of her breasts as he held on to her and she felt herself lifted and swung back again on to the rocky surface of the path and away from the shaky panels of the bridge. She felt that if he let her go, she would sink to the ground, but he held her close and she could feel the hard muscles of his chest almost as if it were part of her own body.

'Little fool,' he murmured harshly into her ear. 'What on earth possessed you to run on such a dangerous path? And stop weeping. I can't stand women who cry.'

She shrugged away from his hold and stood trembling on her own two feet.

'That's a great pity,' she retorted. 'Because it doesn't

matter to me whether you can stand tears or not. I've a perfect right to cry if I want to.'

But now she was too angry with him for tears. Why did he always have this effect on her? He had just rescued her from certain injury and yet she could not be properly grateful.

'You had no right to run away as you did and place yourself in danger. Cliffs are not places to play with just because you feel you must exert your own will against mine. Suppose I had been forced to drop you? How do you think I would have felt? And all because you were determined to thwart my good intentions.'

'Good intentions?' cried Sophie indignantly. 'You have no good intentions towards me at all. You are only thinking of your own wishes. You haven't given a thought to mine.'

'Oh, yes, I have. If you would consider it at all instead of acting in such a damned obstinate fashion, you would realise that you could be much happier, you and your friends who will possibly come here on vacation, if you were to have a house at the coast instead of a tumbledown *mas* in the middle of nowhere.'

'Well, if you think so little of it, why do you want it? And for that matter, why do *you* choose to live in the middle of nowhere, as you put it?'

'It is my home. The place where I was born, the place that I always came back to however far I wandered around the world. And what's more it suits my purpose to live in an isolated fashion, but that's another story and no concern of yours. Suffice it to say that I would prefer to possess the *mas* myself and not have you letting it out to anyone who chooses to come there.'

'Are you implying that I would rent it to any kind of riff-raff? You are not very complimentary to me or my friends.'

Fabien sighed.

'I am not implying anything of the sort but I value my isolation. I don't want anyone intruding who might be curious about my present way of living.'

'And why should you think strangers would be interested in you, *M. le Comte*?'

Sophie said this scornfully though she knew full well what he was getting at. He obviously did not want anyone to try to find out why he was leading the hermit-like existence that he had now as opposed to the playboy image he had once held. Not that one could see any man as a hermit with Rosine around, she thought ruefully.

'From past experience, I realise they usually are interested, and I do not want that kind of attention. Not ever again.'

He gave a deep sigh and then suddenly seemed to make an effort to shake off his mood.

'But come, Sophie, let's find somewhere where you can clean up and then we'll take lunch in a place I hope you will like. We'll forget the *agence immobilière* for the moment. It seems you, how shall we say, have won the first round.'

'It was you, not I, who chose to make this a fight,' Sophie told him. 'All I want is to be left in peace to follow my plans to renovate my own property. I never asked for your interference.'

She felt bruised and shaken and wished she had not reacted so violently to his efforts to interest her in inspecting houses here. What did it matter? she thought. She could have said no to him, surely? But with his persuasive charm, he was difficult to refuse. Oh, no, she thought, she mustn't start thinking along those lines, for that was what he wanted.

They found somewhere to wash and, after she had done this, brushed her hair and cleaned the sand from her dress, she felt better. She wondered where he intended they should have lunch. A place he hoped she would like? Did he mean he was going to take her to some splendid restaurant? She rather hoped not.

But he took her back to the car and they drove away

from Collioure on curving roads until they were up above the sea with a magnificent view of the coastline. Below them it swept on with bays and inlets making a glorious panorama as far as the eye could see.

'How do you feel about having our *déjeuner* with this view below us? From here you can see as far as the Spanish border, but we can find shade I hope in this grove. Bernadette, our housekeeper, packed us a lunch that I hope you will enjoy. She will be very disappointed if you leave any of it.'

'I don't expect I will.'

'So. Your fight with me has made you hungry, Mademoiselle Sophie?'

'I don't ever choose to fight, so let's forget our differences for a little while, shall we?' Sophie suggested.

She eyed the long slim bottle of wine that he had produced from a cool bag and thought that possibly if she could lull him into a better mood she might learn something to her advantage about his previous adventures.

'Willingly. I'm hoping to enjoy my lunch too. A glass of wine, a loaf of bread and thou beside me singing in the wilderness, but I hope Bernadette has provided us with something better than a crust of bread and I have yet to hear you sing, Sophie.'

'Maybe after the glass of wine,' she said laughing.

'Ah, that's better. Do you know that your smile lights up those amethyst eyes in an altogether delightful fashion?'

'I only know that you are very good at flattery, *M. le Comte.*'

'Fabien, if you please. Why this formality all of a sudden?'

Sophie could not help feeling happy now. However annoying her companion had been, she was charmed by the beauty of the scene, the warmth of the sun, the gentle breeze that was cooling the air under the grove of cork trees high up on the mountainside. They were peculiar trees with a rough red bark from which the cork was harvested. These strange surroundings seemed to Sophie to be all of a piece with the foreign place in which she had spent the last few days, far away from her accustomed life in London. And Fabien himself. How different he was, she reflected, from the men she knew from her place of work, men who treated her as an equal, not as a petulant, annoying child. And yet what charm he could show when he smiled at her as he was doing now, pouring out the greenish-gold wine into long bell-shaped glasses that had been carefully wrapped in a napkin.

He had unrolled a mat and, piling it with gaily coloured cushions, sat like some Eastern potentate, lolling back in comfort and drinking his wine which was accompanied by delicious titbits, spicy rice rolled in tiny pieces of vine leaves, small peppery sausages, plump black olives and little rolls of smoked salmon. This was followed by thick slices of some beautifully prepared ham and various salads that seemed strange and delicious to Sophie, all with slices of fresh fragrant bread. Luscious dried figs were accompanied by small heart-shaped cream cheeses.

'Sorry I can't give you fresh figs, but you have come at the wrong time of year for that. Our best time for fruit is in late September. You should have come then when you could have enjoyed peaches, apricots, figs, grapes.'

'I hope to be able to come at that time too. But, after the English winter, it is wonderful to be here right now with this wonderful sunshine and this marvellous view.

The wine, the delicious food, the warm sunshine all lulled Sophie into a good mood. She forgot her annoyance with Fabien who was now proving a charming companion, teasing her and encouraging her to talk about herself, a quite different proposition from the angry man who had hauled her out of danger. She thought, however, that she should not be talking about herself, for the whole aim and object of being with Fabien was to get his story.

'You seem determined to show me the coastal scenery,' she said now. 'But I understand the mountains are glorious in this part of the world. I've seen Canigou of course, the way it dominates the whole valley, but I have been told that there are terrific gorges and very high mountains all around. I have done some climbing but only in the Lake District of England, in Cumbria, and quite a long time ago when I was at college. Some of it was quite difficult but I've never attempted anything in conditions as rugged as in Switzerland, for instance. Have you ever had any interest in that kind of pastime?'

She felt a little ashamed of pretending such innocence about his past but it seemed the only way in which she could get any information from him. As it was his expression seemed to her to have darkened, but then he seemed to pull himself together again and face her with that charming smile that seemed capable of hiding any other kind of emotion.

'Pastime? I find that an odd word, Sophie, to use for something that was once an integral part of my life.'

Sophie felt a stirring of excitement. She seemed to have somehow struck a chord of communication with him. She must go carefully. It was like trying to play a fish, a large silver salmon, a king of fish, tempting it with a lure until at last it ventured to take the bait.

'Do you mean that you used to do a lot of climbing?' she asked innocently.

He laughed. He was obviously amused and perhaps relieved that she apparently knew nothing of his previous reputation.

'Yes, I did a great deal. It's something I don't care to speak about very often.'

The shadow that had passed over his face seemed to vanish and it was almost as if a cloud had passed over the sun but now there was a return of the radiant day. His brilliant gaze rested on her and he took her hand in his. She could feel his slender, strong fingers tapping a kind of percussive beat on the palm of her hand as if he suffered some kind of nervous stress, but she thought he hardly knew he was doing this for he seemed to be somewhere far away.

'But after all, what does it matter? It is all so long ago and the public have forgotten all about the episode that they thought at the time merited so much adverse publicity.'

'Is that what you meant when you said you didn't believe in looking back?' Sophie asked.

She felt very excited. Was he, she wondered, going to tell her more about that long-dead tragedy?

'Yes, I have always held to that opinion but perhaps sometimes it might be good to break one's silence and confide in a stranger, just as people occasionally tell the story of their life to someone on a train, someone they think they will never meet again.'

'Am I that stranger?' Sophie asked rather breathlessly.

'We could call you that, an innocent person who knows nothing of my past, who is not even interested in it, who will never be even remotely concerned with my life, the way I live now, who, in a few short weeks, will be gone only to return at short intervals if ever. That's the kind of person one could confide in. Maybe it would rid me of the burden of guilt that has pursued me for all these years.'

Suddenly he seemed to arouse himself from a dream, or was it a nightmare, Sophie wondered.

'But that's all nonsense, Sophie. You can't possibly know or have any interest in what I'm talking about. It's of no consequence to our present situation, sitting as I am above the blue Mediterranean on a wonderful day with a beautiful woman who certainly would not wish to hear any awful confessions about a past that is long dead and gone.'

The significant moment had passed. Now Fabien's arm was around her waist, his long fingers seeming to burn through the thin fabric of her dress. She could feel his warm breath on her cheek. If she turned, their mouths would be at kissing distance, but she kept her face obstinately turned aside.

'But I am very interested,' she said, sounding innocent, as if she had not realised he was about to kiss her. 'Climbing mountains is a subject that interests me very much.'

'Some other time, perhaps,' he told her and, taking her face in his hand, he turned her towards him and, before she could stop him, his lips were upon hers and she was swept up in a deep long kiss.

'Much more interesting than the subject of mountains, Sophie, don't you agree?'

His hands were on her shoulder now, slipping the shoe-string strap from it and gently cupping the curve of her breast. She sensed the power of him and was tempted to submit to the enchantment of this blue day, in the grove of strange trees, where the only sound in this sleepy afternoon was the musical chirruping of a cricket and the monotonous call of a hoopoe somewhere in the distance.

But this sort of thing wasn't in the contract she had made with herself when she had vowed to get the story of his life from him. Decidedly she removed his hand and tore herself away from the sensuous temptation of those mobile lips upon her own.

'I would prefer to talk about mountains, Fabien,' she told him. 'We have too short an acquaintance for this.'

He laughed, but made no attempt to hold her again.

'Time has nothing to do with it,' he said, 'when two people find each other attractive. If I had known you a hundred years, Sophie, would it feel any better to be in this beautiful place far away from the crowds? No, it is far more alluring to find oneself charmed by a stranger, and Sophie, you must know I find you extraordinarily attractive with those beautiful violet eyes. What knowledge, I wonder, lies behind that expression that somehow I find too innocent to be true. No girl who has made her career in London could be as naïve as you seem to want to appear.'

His remark was too near the truth for comfort. She had told small white lies about her life, informing him that she did secretarial work and she had pretended she knew nothing of his previous history of mountaineering. But his dark eyes seemed to be watching her every expression, his keen mind penetrating into her very thoughts. Her mouth felt bruised by his kisses, yet she thought she could so easily have accepted his embraces, up here on the mountainside among the strangely beautiful trees underneath the vivid blue sky where somewhere far away a skylark was singing its heart out.

CHAPTER FOUR

Sophie had not managed to get any more information from Fabien during the rest of the afternoon, but still she felt hopeful that one day he would confide in her. He had seemed so near to doing that, and at the last moment had been distracted by the sensuous, amorous atmosphere of the lovely day. Yet, when she had turned away from the temptation to submit to his warm embraces, he had accepted her decision and taken her further along the coast where there were other attractive resorts.

At the old harbour of Port Vendres they sat in their car where an obelisk of rose-coloured marble decorated with fleur-de-lys designs dominated the open space, giving on to the sea and below them old fishing boats with dark red and brown sails lay sheltered. Then there was Banyuls, built around one of the Mediterranean's most perfect bays with its monument to the dead at the very end of an escarpment that fell plunging into the sea.

'You'll notice how the grapevines come almost down to the sea here,' Fabien told Sophie and, as they drove higher away from the place, she could see wave upon wave of fresh young vines covering the hillsides with far below the red roofs of the little town encircling the blue of the bay with its rows of boats ranged along the yacht port.

He had not pressed her further on the subject of looking for a house on the coast but all the same she felt he was trying to impress her with the attractions of the small resorts that were so unspoiled compared with the bigger places of the French Riviera. It was true that if she had been looking for somewhere to live and had not had the *mas* left to her, she would have been tempted to investigate the possibilities of the Cote Vermeille as he called it. But the *mas* was hers already to do with as she liked.

She felt very possessive about it. Fabien, for all his charm, was not to divert her from its renovation. Tomorrow, she thought, she would make another attempt to find someone to help her effect the repairs. Meanwhile this day had given her some ideas, however scanty, about Fabien's personality and she could begin to make notes for her article even if she had not found out as much as she had hoped. He had seemed inclined to confide in her. It only needed more time. If she were to get him in a relaxed mood again, she was sure she could get the information she needed.

But she did not ask him to come in when he brought her back to the house.

'Think it over, Sophie,' he said. 'Dream about the lovely places we have seen today and try to compare them with the *mas*, which you must admit needs plenty doing to it.'

He looked disparagingly at the house with its holes in the roof and the grounds that were high with a thick growth of weeds in spite of her efforts of the day before.

'Of course that's so,' she cried. 'I know that well enough and I intend to do it. You see the broken tiles, the overgrown garden, but I can visualise how it is going to be and it's no use trying to stop me because I'm absolutely determined to do it, even if I have to start the repairs on my own. The first thing I am going to do is to look for those pictures, for I can understand now that if I were to sell some of them it could be a great help. If I had more money, I could bring in labour from further afield and I needn't rely on the workmen of the village who seem all so absolutely loyal to you. Really, you carry on in a most feudal fashion, Fabien. One would think the revolution had never happened.'

He smiled but said nothing and helped her from the car. His hands slipped along her bare arms and then with one hand he turned her face up towards him. She thought he intended to kiss her on both cheeks in the French manner but his arms went around her and he held her so closely that she could feel the throbbing of his heart against her breast. In his dark eyes before he kissed her she imagined she could see a flicker of desire that was ready to glow into a flame if she so much as responded and she tried to withstand the frightening thrill of excitement that threatened to set her body alight in response to the fire that was kindled in his.

With difficulty she thrust herself away from him and went to stand on the broken steps at a safe distance. But here she was on a level with his mouth and she could see his confident smile as he stood a couple of yards away, ready to take her in his arms again.

'Goodbye, Fabien,' she cried hastily. 'Thank you for the lovely day. It was glorious even if you didn't get your wish.'

'That depends what my wish was, doesn't it?' he told her. His laughter rang out now deep and strong from somewhere in that strongly muscled chest. 'A kiss can make up for any number of disappointments so long as it is done with the right person. And who knows? I may have sown the seeds of various plans today so you mustn't say goodbye in that cold English way for it's surely *au revoir*, Sophie.'

'You are incorrigible,' she shouted as he turned to stride back to the car. 'You haven't changed my mind about the *mas*, so be sure of that, Fabien.'

'But I hope to change your mind about a number of other things, Sophie, before I am through with you,' he called, and, thrusting his long legs over the low door of the sports car, he switched on the ignition and with a roar was away down the rough road that led from the *mas*.

She watched his dark head until the car was only a silver streak eating up the distance that lay between the *mas* and the château. She thought he would stop at nothing to get his own way and buy the *mas* from her, he would even seduce her if she were willing, but she was not to be charmed so easily. All the same, he makes love very attractively, she thought. What would it be like if . . . but no, she mustn't think of that.

As she turned into the house, she saw that night was

coming fast and there were dusky shadows under the ghostly radiance of the flowering cherries. Something flew with a weird cry from the gap in the roof, making her start with shock until she realised that it was only her old friend the owl, the one she had noticed yesterday. Old friend? She could not imagine she had only been here two whole days. It seemed much longer since she had come to the *mas* and made the acquaintance of Fabian, M. le Comte de Cressac.

As she picked her way carefully over the broken stones of the patio and swung open the heavy creaking door into the dark interior of the cottage, she wondered why he should be so keen to thwart her in her intention to make the *mas* fit to live in for herself and her friends. But that was just it, she thought. He didn't want anyone to be near enough to disturb his way of life, though certainly he did not appear to want to live like a monk. No. He wanted to live like a nobleman of long ago, a count or a king who had *Droit de Seigneur* over any pretty girl he happened to fancy. King of Catalonia, she thought. That's what I'll call him in my own mind.

She had taken the precaution of buying a fresh baguette on the way home and now she made herself a supper of bread and goat's cheese and a salad of tomatoes and chives which she had noticed flourishing amongst the weeds, flowering with pretty purple heads. She made herself some strong coffee, for she was determined that in spite of feeling a little drowsy after her day in the sun, she would stay up and make notes on everything she had observed today of Fabien's personality.

She lit the oil lamp and it cast a pool of light over the old worn table, leaving shadows in the corners of the room except where the fire leaped up in cheerful flames. Those logs would not last for ever, she thought now, and how was she to manage to cut the wood that was all around the *mas* if she could not get any help? Surely in this village there must be someone willing to work for her, someone who had not been persuaded into working for the Count? It would be more costly if she had to employ someone from a nearby town and not so convenient. She tried not to think about these problems and to make preparations to make her notes. She had brought a portable typewriter and now sat down and, slipping a piece of paper into it, she tried to concentrate on putting down her opinion of Fabien.

It was not difficult to think about him, she found, but puzzling. How to reconcile the man who they said had chosen to cut himself off from the world with the charming companion who had entertained her and made love to her so skilfully on this dazzling day of a French spring? But then she thought how the old aunts, Germaine and Belle, had said that he always got what he desired, always had his own way. Well, for once he's not going to do that, she vowed.

She prepared her notes under various headings just to make a start. Appearance, she wrote, and at once she could see him almost too clearly from the shining black hair, dark flashing eyes long lashed under quizzical brows, aquiline, proud profile, mocking smile from those mobile lips that seemed to promise passion, tall whipcord frame with broad shoulders and narrow hips, oh, yes, he moved like a dancer or maybe with the agility of a bullfighter in spite of that slight limp.

Character, she wrote. This was not as easy. How could one understand such a man on two days' acquaintance? She had found him arrogant, selfish, feudal in his outlook, too sure of himself as regards women, but on the other hand with what a lot of charm he had made love to her, how difficult it had been to refuse him.

When Sophie found herself writing in this way, she tore the page out and, crumpling it up, flung it on the fire. She would imply in her article that he was a womaniser but there were to be no personal details. Moody, she wrote. Obviously harks back to that tragedy although it all happened so long ago. Considering this, there must have been some deep psychological injury to have such an effect

on a previous playboy of a man. It was the story of this
episode that she must get from him. He had seemed almost
on the verge of telling her something and had then drawn
back. If she encouraged him, perhaps he would feel more
inclined to tell her about it when the opportunity arose. He
had said that sometimes one could tell things to a stranger
that one could not confide to a more intimate friend. And
she was a stranger to him and likely to remain so too in spite
of his kisses, for she had discovered in two days that he was a
hard man to get to know.

She was so absorbed in her thoughts on the subject of
Fabien that for a long time she had been unconscious of her
surroundings. The oil lamp cast a pool of light burnishing
her bright hair, but beyond this the room was dark and odd
shadows leapt among the old rafters of the roof. The fire
had burned low and the noise that startled her out of her
deep concentration seemed to her at first to come from the
falling of a burned-out log. With difficulty she brought
herself back to the present and went to replenish the fire.
But there it was again and definitely this time it had
nothing to do with the fireplace. It had come from down
below in the cellar, a sound as if something had been
dislodged there.

Could it be the wind that had caused it? But the night,
when she glanced out of the window, was very still and the
cherry trees stood like white ghosts of trees silvery in the
moonlight, the blossom undisturbed. More of the noise. She
knew the owl was in the roof but this sounded as if it came
from the cellar directly underneath her. Possibly a cat or
some other stray animal was looking for a place to rest
during the night, but she had better go and investigate. She
looked at her wrist-watch. Midnight. She had been
working for a longer time than she had realised. It was time
she was in bed if she was to do all the things she intended
tomorrow. But first she thought she had better find out
what was causing the noises in the cellar. Otherwise she
might be disturbed during the night.

Taking a torch in her hand, she opened the heavy door, crossed the patio and descended the broken steps that led to the cellar. This was part of her domain that she had not yet inspected and now, through the shadowed darkness of the ruined doorway, it looked rather daunting, not the place to search at night with strange sounds still coming from somewhere in that black interior now that she was standing quietly. There seemed to be a kind of glow coming from behind that thick pillar that supported the upper floor. Surely not the start of a fire? By now thoroughly alarmed, she hastened across the rough flags, her torch only lighting the area immediately in front of her, and, as she came around the corner of the pillar, she gasped in surprise and shock.

'What are you doing here?' she cried, remembering to speak in French.

Sitting very much at his ease was a dark, thick-set man dressed in worn denim jeans and a rough black jersey. He had an ancient battered chair for a seat and was manipulating a small cooker with a gas cylinder on top of which was a pot from which issued very savoury smells of herbs and some kind of meat.

At the sight of her, he sprang up and swept off his black beret revealing a mop of black curls rising from his head almost in an Afro style, but he didn't seem the least perturbed at being discovered on her property, she thought.

'*Mademoiselle, enchanté,*' he cried.

He had an odd kind of accent, she thought. Maybe he was a Catalan?

'But who are you and what are you doing here?' she demanded. 'What do you want?'

It seemed ironic, she thought, that twice she had been confronted by a man who had no right to be here, when all she herself wanted was to be left in peace to get on with the task of renovating her property. Should she be afraid of this large man who looked so strong? She felt her heart beating quickly in her breast as she waited for his reply. He looked so fierce and wild like some gipsy who had strayed from his tribe, and if he had come to rob her or worse she held out little hope of being able to fight with him.

'Vidal le Garrec at your service, *mademoiselle*.' A wicked looking grin illuminated his face making him look even more fearsome. 'As for what I'm doing, I'm cooking my supper, one of *M. le Comte's* rabbits. He has plenty so he can spare one for me even if he wouldn't think so.'

Sophie thought so far he didn't seem as if he intended her any harm and his feelings on the subject of Fabien seemed to coincide with her own.

'It smells delicious,' she said, forgetting her fear.

'If *mademoiselle* would honour me?'

He produced an enamel plate and, shovelling some of the contents of the stewpot on to it, he offered her a broken cane seat, in the meanwhile pouring a mug of red wine for her.

She must be mad, thought Sophie, to sit down with this fierce strange man, but she found herself obediently spooning up the savoury stew and drinking the raw red wine, and wiping her plate with a hunk of bread.

'Not the finest of wines, *mademoiselle*, but all I can afford since the *Comte* dispensed with my services.'

'You mean the Count has dismissed you?' asked Sophie, her quick brain alert to the implications of this. 'What is it you do?'

'I'm a *maçon*, *mademoiselle*, the finest *maçon* in the district. My speciality is *le faience*, I can tile better than anyone in the Roussillon, but if I'm given the chance I can turn my hand to any kind of building. *Hélas*, there is little work going on in the district and, since my dispute with the Count, there is even less future for me. I was turned out of my lodgings because I was unable to pay the rent and since then I have been living by my wits.'

Sophie thought he might do quite well by his wits, for he didn't look as if they were lacking. He had a bright, intelligent face, wicked perhaps and headstrong, but not evil. She could imagine that this kind of personality might clash with the arrogant character of the Count.

'But not to worry, *mademoiselle*. I'm off tomorrow. I won't trouble you any more. I saw you arrive and made myself scarce but I came back tonight to fetch my things, and being hungry, I could not resist cooking the rabbit I had caught. I thought you would have been asleep long ago.'

'Have you got some work elsewhere then?'

'No, but I'm leaving the district and going to try to find work somewhere else. I'll miss it here because I'm a Catalan in spite of the fact that my mother was English. Maybe I'll try to find work in Spain. It's no good trying to find anything here now that the Count has turned against me.'

'But I'm not against you, M. le Garrec,' said Sophie.

He gave a great hoot of laughter.

'That's *très gentille*, Mademoiselle, especially considering I have taken over your cellar. You can call me Vidal. I'm not used to formality. But what do you mean by saying you are not against me?'

'I mean that I need someone to help me renovate the *mas*. Would you be able to do that, do you think?'

Vidal gave another great shout of laughter that seemed to come from the deep barrel of his chest. His hands were flung out and he seemed to Sophie very foreign, very French.

'Of course,' he said. 'Nothing easier, but I warn you, Mademoiselle, *M. le Comte* isn't going to like it.'

'It doesn't matter to me whether the *Comte* likes it or not. Why exactly did you leave his service?'

Almost too late Sophie realised that she had not asked this wild-looking character what had caused his dismissal. If he were as good a workman as he boasted, there must have been some misdemeanour of a serious nature to make Fabien get rid of him. She had been so excited at the prospect of at last getting someone who would work for her that she had not thought further than that.

'Nothing to do with my work, *mademoiselle*, if that is what you are thinking. It was more personal, more a matter of character. *M. le Comte* and I both like our own way and there was some trouble concerning a woman, but I won't go into that.'

Sophie thought it might be discreet not to enquire about his last statement too closely.

'But I must warn you, M. le Garrec, that I too am accustomed to getting my own way,' she told him.

Another great bellow of laughter.

'You, *mademoiselle*? *Eh bien*, maybe that figures, because you are a *rouquine*, a redhead, *n'est-ce pas*? Such women usually have strong wills, but I like a woman of temperament. I feel we could get on well together.'

Sophie felt this too but she hesitated to say so in case she should appear too enthusiastic. She was thrilled at the idea of having found someone to work for her after all her frustrations. Let Fabien be annoyed. What did it matter? He had been no help to her at all. In fact he had deliberately set out to hinder her.

'You can sleep here tonight,' she told Vidal. 'And we'll decide what is to be done in the morning. I cannot pay very high wages but I'll pay you what is considered fair here.'

'As long as I have a roof over my head and enough to buy food and wine, I'll be happy to work for you, *mademoiselle*. Doubtless I could earn higher wages if I travelled further but this is my own country, and I want to stay here.'

'How is it that you can speak English?' asked Sophie curiously.

'My father was in the *maquis*, the resistance, and had to escape to England, eventually spending some time there. He married an English girl and after the war they came back here where I was born. They are both dead now but I learned to speak English from my mother.'

'Now I understand. That is fortunate for me. Let's sleep on it and we'll discuss things in the morning. Good night, Vidal.'

'Good night, *mademoiselle, dormez bien.*'

Almost immediately on her return to the house, Sophie fell into a dreamless sleep. It had been a long exciting day and tonight she did not hear the owls calling or the mice rustling in the roof or the squeak of bats darting for moths around the white blossom of the cherry-trees. She was in her own house and she was going to remain here. She now had someone to help her and Fabien would never persuade her to part with it.

Next morning it seemed to her that the sun had only just risen when she was ready to start work, but Vidal was even earlier. To her delight he had already gone into the village and returned with baguettes and hot croissants. French bakers must work all night, she thought, as she drank her bowl of hot coffee and enjoyed the hot crispy crescents of flaky bread with some strawberry jam that she had purchased previously. Then she was ready to start, feeling brimming with energy.

She was surprised to find that Vidal had already started and was busy clearing the broken pavement of the patio, but when he saw her he threw down the rusty tool he had doubtless found in the cellar and came towards her grinning broadly.

'Bonjour, mademoiselle, comment ça va?'

After greeting him, Sophie explained that they had better do a general survey on what should be done to the mas.

'I am not rich,' she told him. 'So if you know of any way to get building materials cheaply, I'd be glad of that. They must be good though. I want everything to be of reasonably good quality.'

'Leave it to me, Mademoiselle Rouquine. I know where I can get the best and at a low price too.'

Sophie thought that somehow she was willing to trust him, this rough, wild-looking man with the sinister hooked nose and wicked grin. Maybe it was just that she felt desperate to get someone to do the work on the mas, but, no, it wasn't just that. There was something that appealed to her about Vidal even if he did look like a bandit.

'I know where I can borrow a truck to fetch the building materials,' Vidal told her.

'I don't want anything to look modern,' Sophie told him. 'Everything must look as it did when the *mas* was built, except that I want a heating system for the water.'

'Leave it to me, *mademoiselle*. I know what the old Catalan houses looked like. You shall have a tiled ceiling equal to anyone's in Roussillon.'

'But won't that cost a lot?'

'I know where to get materials dirt cheap, but good quality, never fear. This is going to be a house you may be proud of. When you have Vidal le Garrec helping you, you may know there'll be good workmanship in every detail, and when *M. le Comte* sees it, he will regret our little quarrel.'

Sophie wondered how far Vidal's enthusiasm about repairing the *mas* was due to a wish to get even with Fabien. But he did not know that Fabien wished to buy the *mas*. Or did he? News travelled fast in a village. Maybe the whole place knew by this time that Fabien wished her to buy something else, especially as he had employed all the available people to work for him before she had been able to engage them.

'I'll need a helper,' Vidal announced now.

Sophie's heart sank. She thought this had all been too good to be true. Now he was going to demand that his friends should be employed too, probably at some high rate. But her suspicions were not justified.

'I know of a good workman. Because of his lack of wits, he has difficulty finding employment but I can get along with him well. His name is Pujol and we can get his help for next to nothing. He'll be glad of food and shelter and he can help me by carrying bricks and so on.'

'Won't anyone object to that?' cried Sophie, thinking of unions and trade regulations.

'Bless you, no. We'll be doing the boy a charity employing him.'

Sophie felt she was being carried away on the wave of Vidal's enthusiasm. Was she being foolish to trust her precious *mas* to the ministrations of this rough-looking fellow? But what alternative did she have? She must take a chance on it.

After he had made a thorough inspection of the house, he went off to negotiate about the truck and the building materials and was back again in a surprisingly short space of time with an ancient vehicle upon which rose-coloured bricks were piled. They were of exactly the right shade and there were also grey tiles for the roof. On top of these, sitting very precariously, was a young man who looked at first sight like a scarecrow from the fields. He had long blond hair, a russet wind-baked skin and blue eyes that gazed dreamily around him. He wore very ragged denim jeans, an old T-shirt adorned with his own name and a battered hat. This, Vidal informed her, was Pujol, and the young boy greeted her shyly.

It did not take long for Vidal to get them started on the work of repairing the brickwork. This had seemed to Sophie the most important task to start first, although there was so much to do that she herself hardly knew where to start. She would do some cleaning herself of the interior and one of her first tasks must be to look for the missing pictures. From outside there came the clink of trowels and bursts of song of a rather ribald nature but she did not mind, for she was happy to have the noise of work going on in place of the frustrations she had felt yesterday.

Now to look for the missing paintings. The most obvious place where they might be was the studio in the loft where Aristide had done his work. There was a ladder, somewhat fragile, that let down from a trap door, and gingerly she began to climb up this. She found herself in a room with sloping ceiling and sturdy wooden beams. A whole tree-trunk seemed to support the roof from one end of the building to the other. A window in the roof was now shuttered. It must have been added to give light for Aristide's painting, but Sophie did not need to unfasten the shutters, for light poured in from the places where slates were missing. With a nervous start, Sophie realised that the owl was watching her from its perch in a corner of the room, gazing at her with huge dark eyes. She hoped it was too sleepy after its night's hunting to be disturbed by her presence.

Everything was thick with dust and littered with dried leaves and the debris of last autumn and winter, but around her she could see the remains of Aristide's profession, a couple of easels with unfinished works on them, now hard to decipher because they were ruined by the winter's storms. There were old paintbrushes and dried up paints and palettes, but Sophie looked in vain here for any sign of the missing paintings. Just as well really, she thought, for they would have been ruined by now in these conditions. In a drawer however she found some pleasing sketches, small things unfinished that could not have much value to anyone but herself. However, she was glad to have them and descended the ladder with them grasped carefully in her hand. It was no use, she thought, even attempting to clean up the studio until the roof was repaired. It would be much better to start investigating the rest of the house.

She had just decided that the cellar was the place she would have to look at next when she heard the sound of a car coming up the driveway, changing into a louder lower gear as it negotiated the bumps in the roadway. Her heart began to beat rather more quickly. Could it be Fabien? But no. As she looked out at the same time trying to shake off the dust of the studio from her person and, feeling conscious that there were dried leaves in her tangled hair and possibly smudges of dirt on her face from her black hands, she saw Rosine stepping out of a bright yellow sports-car, her dark sweep of hair silky on her shoulders, her tangerine jumpsuit clinging to her figure in all the right places, the thin straps of her white patent pumps leaving her heels bare above the three-inch stiletto heels.

Rosine however had no eyes for Sophie, who was still in the darkness of the doorway. Her look was fixed on Vidal and his companion and she strode across to him and addressed him in a torrent of French which Sophie found totally impossible to understand. In response to this Vidal laid down his trowel and seemed to answer her with few words, but what he said seemed to infuriate her. She tossed her head, her black mane of hair spreading around her beautiful face like a waterfall, and her voice rose higher as she seemed to whip herself into a fury, but Vidal responded calmly, shrugging his shoulders and looking down at her from his great height like a large Labrador dog being disturbed by a French poodle.

Frustrated, she turned on her high heels, losing a shoe in the process, and picked her way over the rubble to the door where Sophie was standing watching the scene.

'*Bonjour*, Sophie,' she exclaimed. 'I came to enquire how you were getting on, whether you had found somewhere more suitable, when Fabien gave up his time to take you to the coast, and here I find this *espèce de canaille* who says he is working for you.'

'Yes, Rosine,' Sophie replied, trying to sound calm although she could feel rage bubbling up inside her. 'Vidal has promised to help me to do the repairs needed to make the place habitable.'

'But you cannot have realised who he is. Fabien was forced to dismiss him from his service because he was the most insolent and arrogant man one could imagine.'

'Nevertheless I feel I can get on with him' Sophie replied. 'And as for arrogance, I do not have to imagine arrogance. There is plenty of it around here as far as I can see.'

'Fabien will not be pleased if you insist on employing this man.'

Sophie lifted her chin. Her copper hair glinted in the sunshine. Vidal had not called her *la Rouquine* for nothing.

'It does not concern me in the least, Rosine, whether Fabien is pleased or not. My only aim is to get the *mas* repaired with the least possible interference from outsiders.'

'Outsiders? How can you possibly call Fabien that when he has a right to be allowed to buy the *mas*. It is you who are the outsider, you who have come from England to disturb Fabien's life-style.'

'Hardly that, Rosine. Fabien need have nothing to do with me if he so wishes. You can hardly accuse me of disturbing his life-style.'

'You intend to live here for part of the year and to bring your friends here too. That will incommode Fabien who likes to live in the manner to which he is accustomed with no curious foreigners around.'

'Why should they be curious? He need have nothing to do with my guests.'

'Oh, you can be sure people will not leave him alone. He was once a very famous person.'

'I think the word is notorious,' Sophie told her. 'And really, Rosine, I do not intend to be driven away from my own property by surrendering to Fabien's wishes. It does not concern me whether he likes me to be here or not. I intend to get this place repaired and to use it as my second home. I am not afraid of Fabien and have no interest in his getting his own way over this. It strikes me he has been too used to everything going his way for far too long. Probably Vidal was dismissed because he put up a bit of opposition, but Fabien cannot dismiss me from here so easily.'

Rosine stamped her foot on the broken pavement and broke the thin strap of her sandal. She gave an exclamation of annoyance.

'There was more to it than that. Vidal was a thorough rogue, as you will find out in time, Sophie. I believe he has been living here since he was dismissed. You had better look out for your belongings. It wouldn't surprise me if you find valuables missing.'

Sophie had a sudden qualm of doubt. Rosine was so

convinced that Vidal was a villain. Suppose her own intuition was wrong and Vidal was a bad lot? He might even have taken the missing pictures. But, no, she was determined not to be bullied by Rosine and Fabien into dispensing with his services.

CHAPTER FIVE

SOPHIE had half expected that Fabien would come storming down to the *mas* when he heard from Rosine that she had employed Vidal, but a few days passed during which the building made good progress and she did not hear from the château. By now she had searched the whole of the house with negative results and she decided to ask at the bank whether they knew if Aristide had deposited them elsewhere. Although Vidal was getting materials at a remarkably low price, the costs were mounting up and Sophie was afraid there might come a time when she would have to call a halt to the repairs if she did not manage to get more funds.

Of course there was the payment for her proposed article on Fabien, which was a much less vague proposition than the value of Aristide's paintings which might or might not exist, but if Fabien was going to ignore her, she would not be able to make much progress with it. Perhaps she had been wrong not to encourage him when he had seemed attracted to her, but she was sure he behaved like this with any pretty woman, and in her case he had had a motive, to try to make her do as he wished with regard to selling the *mas* to him.

At the bank in the village they said they had no knowledge of where Aristide's paintings might be but suggested she should try the Art Gallery at Ceret.

'They have a large number of works by Picasso, Braque, Chagall, Matisse and Miro there. M. Aristide was always most interested in exhibiting his works in that setting. It's possible he left them there.'

'Thank you. I'll try that,' said Sophie with renewed hope.

'Why waste petrol?' said Vidal, when she told him she

was going to Ceret. 'I need to go there to get some materials. I'll take you in there. It's market day and it will save you having to park.'

He dropped her in the centre of town, promising to pick her up later. It was the first time she had been to Ceret, the town that seemed so suitably named in its valley of cherry orchards. She admired the old ramparts encircling the little streets where spring water bubbled in the sunlight, running through the gutters. The water played its cascading song again in small fountains in the squares where on the old houses balconies of wrought iron looked like patterned lace. She tore herself away from the interesting-looking market in the centre and went to look for the museum where she had been told there were cubist pictures displayed.

'Yes, we did have some of M. Aristide's paintings,' the attendant told her. 'But he had reclaimed them some time before he died. There was some talk of his having an exhibition at the château. Have you met *M. le Comte* yet? Perhaps he could help you.'

Fabien? But surely she had mentioned in front of him that she hoped to find the pictures. He could not be concealing them from her, could he? He was capable of doing anything to get his way and prevent her from living in the *mas*. But taking the pictures that belonged to her? If he had them, his idea might be to hold on to them until she had consented to sell the *mas* to him, then he might give them to her when it was too late. She could believe anything of him.

Thanking the attendant for this rather disturbing idea, she made her way back to the market. The stalls were near to the lofty ramparts underneath the tall plane trees. Sophie wandered around enjoying the busy scene, the crowds, the pungent fragrance of fresh vegetables, of herbs and cheese, the smell of newly baked bread and cakes, and of hot doughnuts being cooked on a nearby stall. She stopped to buy one of these *beignets* as she knew they were called, and, receiving one half wrapped in paper, she wandered from

stall to stall munching at the warm, sugary confection that
had a peach in its centre, and enjoying the hot sunshine
filtering through the tall trees on to the busy scene.

She had just finished this and was carefully wiping the
sugar and fat from her fingers when she heard her name
called and saw Rosine and Fabien sitting at a table outside
a café.

'Hi, Sophie,' cried Rosine, lazily stretching beautifully
tanned arms above her head like a cat that has lain too long
in the sun. 'We have been watching you for the last few
minutes, enjoying your *beignet* like a girl let out of school.'

'It's true she looks like a schoolgirl,' Fabien agreed, 'with
that copper-coloured, how do you call it, pony-tail and
those denim jeans and checked shirt.'

Rosine looked anything but a schoolgirl, thought Sophie,
feeling a little embarrassed and conscious that her face was
probably still covered in sticky sugar. Rosine was wearing a
very sophisticated sun-dress in a bright red that left bare
her beautifully brown shoulders. Her hair was looped up in
an intricate style as if she had just visited the hairdresser
and on the nails of her hands and feet was a polish in a
shining translucent shade of gold.

'Sit down and have a drink with us,' Fabien commanded.
Sophie sat and accepted a menthe while Fabien drank his
lager and Rosine had a *citron pressé*.

'What are you doing here in town?' asked Rosine, 'I
thought you would be too busy to visit Ceret when we hear
it is all go at the *mas*.'

'I had some business to attend to,' Sophie told her.

She did not intend to say anything about the paintings
until she got an opportune moment with Fabien on his own,
and she was glad when Rosine excused herself saying she
had more shopping to do. But, looking at her watch, she
found she had very little time before she had to meet Vidal at
the prearranged place. She got up to go but Fabien caught
her hand and forced her to sit down again.

'You are not in such a hurry, Sophie, are you? I have not

seen anything of you lately so don't run away as if you are scared to be alone with me. *Hélas*, I cannot make love to you here on the pavement in all this crowd.'

'Of course I'm not scared of you, Fabien, why should I be?'

His smile was dark and wicked.

'Just a little matter of your engaging a man called Vidal le Garrec to work for you when you knew I would disapprove.'

Sophie's blue eyes flashed and her hair glinted red in the sunlight.

'It is not of the slightest importance to me, Fabien, whether you approve of my choice of workman or not. Vidal is working very well for me. That's all I need to know.'

Fabien shook his head. Now that his smile had vanished, his expression was haughty and his eyes dark and cold.

'It won't last. He is completely unreliable, as I found to my cost. What's more, for an *ouvrier* he is the most proud, bad-tempered, arrogant man you could imagine.'

'That sounds like a description of someone else I know,' said Sophie slyly, 'someone not a thousand miles from here.'

'Meaning me, I suppose, but, Sophie, take my advice, get rid of him or you'll live to regret it. Vidal is full of extreme socialist ideas and makes trouble wherever he finds work.'

'And I should think that doesn't suit *M. le Comte* with his outdated feudalist notions. I suppose you think everything should be now as it was in the eighteenth century before the fall of the Bastille.'

'Certainly I don't expect people who work for me to rouse all the others to rebel against my discipline. Vidal is a trouble-maker. You would be advised to give him a wide berth.'

'He can hardly rouse my workmen to revolt since I only have him and his young workmate who seems to worship him. Thank you for your advice, Fabien, but, since you have taken all the other available workmen away from me,

I feel free to engage Vidal, who so far has made a good impression on me. And now I must go for he'll be waiting for me to take me home.'

But somehow she must have missed Vidal. She waited in vain at the corner where they had arranged to meet. Now what was she to do? It was too far to walk back to the *mas* and she did not know where she could find a taxi. It was too bad of Vidal to let her down when she had just now been so vigorously defending him. She was standing there hesitating, when an all-too-familiar silver sports-car drew up beside her and Fabien leaned out, his aggravating smile brilliant on his bronzed face.

'So your chauffeur has not yet arrived, Sophie?'

'No, he must have been delayed.'

'But I thought you said that you were late. Could it be that he has stayed drinking with his cronies and forgotten all about you? In my experience his ideas of equality don't always extend to women even if he may be working for them.'

'He'll be along any moment now,' Sophie told him, trying to look dignified.

'You think so? Jump in and I'll give you a lift home. Vidal isn't worth wasting your time over. He has probably forgotten all about you.'

Sophie was furious that she had to accept his offer. What could have happened to Vidal? She had been a fool not to bring her own car into town.

'Don't look so cross,' said Fabien, giving her knee a reassuring pat that annoyed her still further. 'Is it such a tragedy to have to drive home with me?'

'Not a tragedy,' she told him. 'Just a bit irritating.'

'You find me irritating? That's too bad, Sophie, for to me you seem very attractive, albeit in a cool English way. However those lapis lazuli eyes combined with red hair and full rosy lips promise that in the right circumstances, the cool English front could drop its veil, to reveal what?'

'You tell me,' said Sophie coldly. 'What?'

'A passion that you did not realise you ever had, leading to an experience that could not be anything but delightful.'

'But not with you, thank you, *M. le Comte*,' Sophie told him in a very definite fashion.

She thought he would be annoyed by her reply but he simply threw back his dark head and laughed in that mocking fashion that told her all her sharp words merely fell back from his hard personality like snowballs hurled at a wall of steel.

'Now since it seems your workman has taken leave of absence this morning, how about coming back to the château for lunch? A swim will give you fresh appetite if it is missing after eating that beignet. The aunts have been asking when they are to see you again. You made quite an impression on them the other day. They are not accustomed to meeting English girls and they were charmed by your accent and appearance. Who wouldn't be?'

Sophie thought that Fabien was laying on the flattery rather thick again but it might be a good idea to go with him. She very much needed to get on with her article for the journal and she was still no nearer to finding out about the tragedy in his past which was the heart of the matter, the key to the personality she hoped to describe.

'I'm not dressed very respectably to meet Germaine and Isabelle again,' she demurred, 'And I don't have a swimming-costume with me.'

'You will find plenty of those in the changing room. Rosine and others usually leave some around for occasions when we decide to swim, and, as for your present dress, the aunts will think it charming for it makes you look very young, very ingenuous, a complete contrast to the sophistication of the Frenchwomen to whom they are accustomed.'

Sophie thought she hardly liked this character of an ingenue that he seemed determined to thrust upon her. Rosine must have encouraged this impression. She was more used to being thought a talented journalist who would stop at nothing to achieve her objective, but maybe there could be some advantage in appearing less sophisticated to him. If she asked innocent questions, she might get the replies she wanted especially if he thought of her as such a simple character.

The swimming-pool at the château was laid out more in the form of an ornamental lake than a conventional pool. It was of oval shape with a pink marble fountain of a naked nymph riding a dolphin in the middle. Below the clear green water tiled mosaics depicted sea creatures, colourful fish and crustaceans and seaweeds. Fabien directed Sophie to the changing-room to find a costume, and went off to inform the aunts that there would be a guest for lunch.

There were about half a dozen swimsuits hung up in the changing-rooms. To Sophie's eyes they all looked equally revealing. She chose one of bright turquoise blue that was so high-cut that it made her legs look even longer and more slender and was cleverly held together with thongs to cover a deep plunging neckline and a low back. There was a long mirror in the changing room and she gasped with surprise when she saw herself. With her long copper hair hanging on her shoulders and her limbs bronzed by the sun, she looked like some girl entering for a beauty contest, and this impression was confirmed by Fabien as she walked out, for he gave a whistle of admiration and, flinging his hands up in a very Gallic gesture, he exclaimed, 'Miss England in person.'

She felt curiously embarrassed by his obvious admiration. It's because his admiration is so physical, she thought. He knows nothing about me really. His flattery is given to the person he sees now, not to the Sophie who has carved herself a career in a difficult field. He knows nothing of that side of me, but I don't want him to know. The longer he is ignorant of the fact that I am a journalist after a story the better.

After the heat of the morning in the town, the pool was delightfully refreshing. In spite of his limp, Fabien swam like a fish, his black hair wet and seal-like on his sleek head. His shoulders were broad above the slim waist, the whole of him bronzed to dark gold, but there were the marks of old scars on his legs and chest and, when Sophie saw these, they gave her a small frisson of fear as if she had come upon part of a forbidden story. But she mustn't feel this barrier, she told herself. It was up to her to get the information from him, not feel as if she dared not try to find out.

They sat on the rim of the fountain while the water gushed deliciously around them. Sophie was conscious of the coolness of his thigh, now becoming warmer in the hot sun, so close to her own. He grasped her chin in one wet hand and looked deeply into her eyes.

'Lovely Sophie, you are as graceful in the water and as beautiful as that sea-nymph,' he murmured.

She slipped away from him and swam to the side of the pool. She thought she had never before encountered a man who could flatter a woman so outrageously. Climbing out of the water, she towelled herself dry and lay on one of the low lounging-chairs that surrounded the pool. The sky above her was a deep blue dotted with tiny clouds, and swallows swooped low catching tiny invisible insects. She seemed to have entered into another existence from her one in London, an existence in which anything could happen.

Fabien hoisted himself out of the pool and came to sit beside her. She watched him as pearly beads of water formed in rainbow colours on the bronze of his body and chased themselves over the muscles of his deep chest. He did not seem aware of her attention but slowly put out a hand and began to stroke her arm where a few golden freckles were scattered on the smoothness of her skin. She felt startled by the shuddering feeling of pleasure that trembled throughout her body, and told herself firmly not to be ridiculous, to feel so much physical reaction when a man merely touched her arm. She was glad of the interruption when a manservant brought an ice-bucket holding a bottle and she was given a long glass of sparkling wine with strawberries floating on top of it.

'Champagne so early in the day!' she exclaimed.

'Why not? The French do not believe, like the English, that champagne is only for high days and holidays. It is the only thing to drink on a day like this after a refreshing swim with a beautiful girl.'

'It certainly tastes gorgeous,' Sophie told him appreciatively.

As she changed back into her jeans and checked shirt, Sophie felt elated. Could it be the effect of the glass of champagne or was it simply that she was at last getting on with the repairs to the *mas* and seemed to be making some headway in her desire to find out more about Fabien? If she could only be alone with him after lunch in the sleepy air of afternoon in an atmosphere that could inspire confidences, she might get material for that profile.

Germaine and Belle greeted her with great pleasure.

'It is so good for us all to have a chance to practise our English,' vowed Germaine. 'Since Aristide has gone, we do not hear it often enough.'

'Dear Aristide,' fluttered Belle. 'His French accent was always quite charming. I used to try to give him lessons. We used to spend hours practising together. Wicked Aristide. He always wanted to learn the naughty phrases from me.'

'That's enough, Belle,' Germaine scolded. 'I'm sure Sophie doesn't want to hear anything bad of her late uncle from you.'

Belle's rose-petal face crinkled anxiously.

'But, Germaine, I don't mean any harm. I want Sophie to know that Aristide and I had great affection for each other.'

'She knows that already, Tante Belle. I have told her of your fondness for Aristide,' said Fabien.

He drew Belle to the table and poured her a glass of wine and, in her interest in what was for lunch, she seemed to forget to talk any more of Aristide.

However after lunch, when they were having coffee on the terrace, Fabien was called away for a while and Sophie took the opportunity to ask the two old ladies about the exhibition that was supposed to have taken place in the château.

'Is it true that Aristide exhibited some of his paintings here at one time?' she asked.

'Oh, yes, certainly,' Germaine told her. 'During the summer we have several open days when the villagers and other visitors can come to look over the château. It was a custom that was started in dear Papa's day and, even though Fabien does not care too much for it, we have kept on. Aristide exhibited some of his paintings on the last occasion we had the open day. I remember that some of them were sold and he did well from it. We were all quite pleased.

'Oh, yes, but Fabien did not approve of Aristide showing those early portraits he had done of me. He hid them away somewhere but Aristide never knew that. A pity not to show them because they were some of his best paintings although I say it myself. I wonder what has happened to them now. There was something about them. Aristide said they must be kept safe but I can't just recall what he said must be done with them.'

'Yes, Belle, we know you thought highly of those paintings,' Germaine put in rather impatiently. 'But now it's time for your siesta. You know you need to rest after lunch for at least two hours and it is later than usual now.'

When Belle had shuffled away on a waft of muguet perfume, Germaine turned to Sophie.

'My poor Belle, you must not pay much heed to what she says about Aristide. As a girl she was very much in love with him, but now in her poor muddled head it has increased out of all proportion.'

'But what happened to these pictures?' asked Sophie eagerly. 'Were they sold, the portraits of Belle?'

Could these be the lost paintings? she wondered.

'No, as far as I know, Aristide still had them. He always vowed they were for him personally and he would never

sell them but then when his pictures increased in value, he
used to joke with Belle and say they were a kind of
insurance against his old age, for they would fetch a lot of
money now.'

'Did he take them back from the château after he had held
the exhibition?' asked Sophie.

'As to that, I don't know. I expect he did. You must ask
Fabien. He would know. He kept these particular pictures
in his apartment while the exhibition was on. He thought it
was not dignified to show pictures of Belle. Aristide never
knew this. He hated to come here to his own shows so never
knew that those paintings had not been exhibited.'

So could they still be there? Sophie wondered, and could
he be keeping them until she consented to sell the *mas* to
him? Then somehow they could be rediscovered and he
would return them to her but it would be too late then. She
would have disposed of the *mas* to him. Could this possibly
be what was in his mind? Otherwise what could have
happened to the paintings?

Germaine grasped her stick of silver and ivory and, with
its help, rose from her chair. She looked, thought Sophie,
with her flowing black dress and lacy cap, like the good
fairy in an old story. At the same time a manservant came
in with a message.

'*M. le Comte* says he expects to be occupied for the next
half-hour. Would Mademoiselle be good enough to wait for
him?'

'Ah, then perhaps you would like to see something of the
château,' Germaine suggested. 'I can show you around if
you would like that.'

'But I hardly like to deprive you of your rest,' Sophie
protested, wishing again that she had brought her own
transport. 'If you would not mind this, I could wander
around on my own. I hardly think I will get lost.'

Germaine seemed relieved at this suggestion. Like most
old ladies, she was probably a creature of habit but had
politely suggested she should forgo her afternoon's rest in

order to entertain her guest.

'Very well, my dear. The formal rooms are all open. Belle's and my apartments are to the left of the main building and Fabien has the upper right wing to himself. Between the wings in the main part of the house joining the two wings is the long gallery. You may find this of interest because most of the old family portraits are there and some other good paintings. *Hélas*, none of Aristide's. He was too modern to mix with the family's art collection.'

She led Sophie up the winding stairway and, after a few words of explanation, left her in the long gallery and walked away to her own apartment, leaning rather heavily on the silver-handled stick but with a back that was still straight and rigid. Sophie wandered through the gallery looking at the portraits. The women were beautiful, the men dark and fierce with a distinct resemblance to Fabien. When they smiled they had that same wicked look, but when they were painted in serious mood, they looked cold, haughty, arrogant, just as Fabien looked when something had annoyed him.

Germaine had told her where Fabien's apartment could be found. It was far away from the rest of the living-quarters of the château. She wondered whether she should risk investigating whether Fabien was keeping the paintings there. At least it might allay the suspicion that was nagging at her mind. He had said he was not going to return for half an hour. That left her plenty of time.

Germaine had pointed out the heavy door of polished wood that led to the other wing of the château. Tentatively she pushed at it and it gave way under her hand, not making a sound. The craftsman who had carved the intricate design upon this door and made it fit had been a master of hanging doors, she thought. A fierce dragon glared down at her as if guarding its master's domain as she sidled quietly through and found herself on the other side in a corridor carpeted with long runners of faded Persian design. The first door she tried led into a kind of study, definitely a man's room, panelled in wood and dominated by a huge desk of massive design. One whole wall was covered with bookshelves. No paintings. Only a few sporting prints and an antique map of the Loire Valley.

Sophie went on. The rooms were only on one side and on the other side of the corridor were windows from which she could see a panorama of garden and vineyard. Far below she thought she could see Fabien's tall figure as he talked to one of the workmen in front of his wretched folly, the summer-house he had decided to build in order to frustrate her plans for the *mas*. She could risk some more exploration, she thought. The next room was more feminine. Probably it had been the Countess's boudoir when there had been a Countess. It was charmingly furnished in blue with garlands of pink roses on the curtains and Aubusson carpet and blue and rose brocade chairs and sofas disposed around a small fireplace with embossed white classical figures on a pink marble ground. The only pictures were those of country scenes, delicate pastel drawings of shepherdesses and paintings that seemed as if they had been done by Watteau.

A door led into a third room. Sophie went to the window in the corridor and looked out to make sure Fabien was still occupied, but he seemed to have disappeared. She thought she had come so far she must risk looking into what she presumed must be his bedroom, so she opened the door. It was a room very much bigger than the previous two. On a kind of raised platform was a bed even larger and more splendid than the one at the *mas*. It had green velvet curtains looped up at each corner with entwined ropes of gold and, above the bed on the frame that encircled it, was an elaborate carving of the family coat of arms. Sophie's feet sank into the cream carpet as she looked at the tapestry hangings that adorned the three walls and the other wall was practically all taken up by the deep curving window that let in the sunlight from floor to ceiling. No pictures here, or could they possibly be concealed under some of the tapestries?

She stepped forward and gently lifted the corner of one of the tapestries. It revealed nothing except that Fabien must have very good domestics, for there was no dust underneath. Everything was perfectly clean and there was no obvious place where paintings, presumably fairly large, could be hidden. That large armoire? It looked big enough to conceal any number of things, but when she opened it there was a fragrance of sandalwood and racks of Fabien's clothes. Feeling embarrassed, she hastily shut it and went back to her inspection of the tapestries and, just as she was about to lift another one from the wall, she heard a sound which even on this warm afternoon sent a chill running through her body.

A door had slammed and light strong footsteps pounded down the corridor so swiftly that even if she had wanted to hide she could not have managed it. She dropped the tapestry and stood there not knowing what to say or do and feeling most horribly embarrassed to be caught red-handed like this.

'So this is where you are, Sophie. I usually find I have to invite lovely women into my bedroom but now I find you here already. What a pleasant surprise! But then I have heard that English women are good at taking the initiative. Was I deceived then by that so innocent apearance?'

He came swiftly towards her and she backed away hurriedly.

'Oh, no, Fabien, you have quite the wrong idea. I did not come into your apartment for this.'

But forced up against the tapestry, she could not withstand him. Now he was holding her in his arms, his mouth close to hers, parted in a mocking smile.

'But why are you here, my sweet Sophie, here in my bedroom, if not for this?'

His lips descended on to hers and she was caught up in a kiss that was strong and savage as if he were punishing her, not at all like the romantic kisses he had given her previously. His hands were on her body, slipping under the shirt and finding the smooth skin of her back. Sophie felt a shuddering response as those long brown fingers sought out the soft curves of her breasts and then, with a great effort of will, she flung herself away from him.

His eyes glittered with mocking laughter and she realised that he was using her, punishing her for being here, for this intrusion into his most private place.

'You must believe me, Fabien, I don't want your lovemaking.'

His eyes were dark, his expression at its most arrogant.

'You could have fooled me, my dearest Sophie. You may look like a little girl but your response to me is that of a woman. So if you did not want me to make love to you on this warm inviting afternoon, what did you want?'

'Germaine suggested I should look around the château. I looked at the pictures in the gallery and then wondered if you had any of Aristide's paintings here.'

There, she had said it, but she had not implied what she had thought, that he might be keeping them according to his own plan of depriving her of them until he could get his way and buy the *mas* from her.

'And why should I have any of Aristide's paintings here?' he demanded.

'You admired his paintings,' she stammered. 'I wondered if you had kept any for yourself.'

His expression was hard, his mouth bitter.

'You mean, don't you, Sophie, that you suspect me of keeping the pictures you say are missing from the *mas*, the pictures which you hope to sell so you can have the repairs done. If you think me capable of theft you have a poor opinion of me. Let me tell you, the de Cressacs have always defended their reputation against anyone who accused them, but I hardly think your suspicion is worth contradicting. If you want to know who has your pictures, look nearer home. What about Vidal? He was living illegally at the *mas* for a long time before your arrival and he is used to living by his wits. He is clever enough to know he could sell those pictures anywhere and hope to make a good profit. Ask him where your pictures are but, take it from me, they are probably in some Paris salon by now being sold for an exorbitant price by a dealer who is not so scrupulous as to refuse stolen goods. That is of course if the pictures ever really existed. They might just have been a figment of Aristide's imagination.'

Could she believe him in anything? Sophie wondered. He seemed so righteously indignant at her suspicions and yet he had played that trick on her before by commandeering all the workmen. He and Vidal were enemies so of course he would accuse him. But it was true that Vidal had had the opportunity to take the pictures if they had been in the house. Yet the *notaire* had said they were missing and he must surely have sought them in the house first. Somehow she could not suspect Vidal, or was it just that she did not want to suspect him when she was getting on with him so well and he was doing such good work?

And she did not want to make an enemy of Fabien if she was to complete the article her editor had commissioned. He was sitting on the bed, his head bowed, as if he had been deeply hurt by her accusation. She went up to him now and put her hand on his shoulder.

'I'm sorry, Fabien, that I suspected you. I see now how wrong I was.'

But did she? It was still just as true that he would stop at nothing to get his own way.

He put up his hand and touched her face. Now his touch was gentle, tender even, completely different from that of the wild lover of a few minutes before. He drew her down to the bed and lay beside her.

'Lovely Sophie, how can I stay angry with you when you smile at me with those astonishing eyes and those lips that promise so much?'

She closed her eyes against the blaze of passion in his, but he kissed the lids and it was as if a butterfly had brushed against her. She felt his hands on the smoothness of her skin, following the curve of her neck to where her breasts divided and then caressing their rosy tips into hardened response. One part of her, the greater part, wanted to relax and let these wonderful sensations take hold of her completely, and yet there was a small, cool place at the back of her mind that was saying, 'Take care, he wants to seduce you, subjugate you to make you submissive to anything he could wish, and his main wish is to get possession of your property.' Sophie thought she must be mad and yet the feeling of being with him in this great down-soft bed was so delicious it was extremely hard to resist, but resist it she must.

She drew away from him and sat up, smoothing the tousled silk of her copper hair, holding him from her with hands firm against the naked bronze of his shoulders.

'Oh, no, Fabien, just because you happen to have caught me in your room, that's no reason why I should allow you to seduce me, pleasant as it might be for you.'

He shrugged aside her hands from his shoulders and sat up, swinging his legs on to the floor, but then his hands came down on either side of her as she lay on the bed and she felt enclosed in a cage of his making. He gave a rather bitter smile and, although part of her wished he would kiss her again, he did not do so but sat there looking at her with an intensity that filled her with confusion. She found she could not meet that dark, sensual gaze.

'Pleasant? Oh, Sophie, it could be more than pleasant, don't you think? It could be a most wonderful experience if you could just forget for a while your cool English ways. But no matter. You have called a halt to something that promised utter delight so there is nothing for it now but to take you home. You may wish to make yourself respectable again after this little foray, while I go to fetch the car, but, Sophie, it was not unprovoked, *n'est-ce pas*? However, I'll let you go this time, though I don't promise to be so forgiving in the future.'

He strode out of the room, his shirt unbuttoned to the waist, a golden amulet swinging on a chain over the dark curling tendrils of his chest.

Sophie was quiet as he drove her back to the *mas*. She felt let down and dissatisfied with the events of the afternoon. She had discovered nothing about the missing paintings except that they were not obviously in Fabien's apartment, and she had laid herself open to his accusation that she had provoked him into making love to her, nor had she discovered anything else about his past history. It was true that somehow in spite of the fact that he could make her furiously angry on occasion, he could be enormously attractive when it came to making love. But it was quite obviously a charming game that he could play. See how quickly he had recovered his poise after she had refused him. That showed it had meant very little to him.

CHAPTER SIX

SOPHIE insisted that Fabien should leave her outside her own grounds. Feeling as disorganised as she did after the events of the afternoon, she did not relish the idea of an encounter between Vidal and Fabien, and the *Comte* could easily be scathing over Vidal's failure to pick her up at the appointed place. Fabien took her decision with relief, she thought. Probably, after this afternoon, he would have nothing more to do with her. As she picked her way over the rough ground, she could not hear the usual sound of cheerful singing that accompanied Vidal's work, but she could see him high on a ladder with Pujol handing bricks beside him.

She strode towards them feeling a surge of resentment that was partly caused by the whole catastrophe of the afternoon. She felt she wanted to vent her feelings on someone and here was Vidal, whose failure to collect her at the appointed place had been the start of her troubles. But when she arrived and could see him properly, she stopped short in dismay. His face was bruised and blackened with some of the skin broken and he had the beginnings of what was obviously going to be a very impressive black eye.

'Vidal, what happened to you?' she cried.

He stopped work and descended the ladder.

'*Je suis désolé, mademoiselle*, that I could not drive you home. As you see, this business delayed me.'

'Oh, never mind about that. I mean what happened to you? What have you done to your face?'

'I didn't do it, *mademoiselle*. Other people did it for me. I was drinking very peaceably in a bar I know in Ceret, when some of the Count's men came and started an argument. What could I do? I had to fight them. I gave as

100

good as I got, I assure you. The others are nursing their wounds also.'

'The Count's men, but who are they?'

'Some of the *ouvriers*, the men who are doing his building. They mocked me for working for a woman and an *étrangère*, a foreigner, so naturally I had to fight them. It's my belief that *M. le Comte* had encouraged them in this. He does not like the notion that I am working for you. As everyone knows, he wants the *mas* for himself.'

Sophie was astonished that this fact seemed to be known to the whole populace. But of course in a district like this, when someone like the Count was involved, one could expect it.

'You had better come inside and I'll give you something for your face,' she told Vidal.

As she helped to dress his bruises, she felt more and more furious that this should have happened, and, when she was alone, she sat down and tried to think things out. Had it been deliberate that Fabien had picked her up and taken her to the château for lunch? Did he know that his men were going to pick a fight with Vidal? And maybe he knew about this all the time he was making love to her, she thought. Oh, how could he? But she had always sensed that he was capable of anything to get his way. Thank heaven she had refused his persuasive lovemaking. She vowed that in future she would not be taken in so easily.

She did not hear from Fabien next day and she thought that there went the chance of completing her article for the journal, but in her present mood she hardly cared. She felt low and humiliated at the way he had tried to use her. When she met him again she would be very cold. His charm had ceased to work for her, she told herself.

In the afternoon, when she was taking a well-earned rest from her strenuous efforts in the garden, she was alarmed to hear the sound of a car engine coming up the stony drive. It was, however, a yellow vehicle that could be glimpsed through the trees and, when it arrived with a screech of tyres and a flurry of sandy dust, Rosine stepped out looking as if she were ready to model in a fashion show. Her flowing dress was of a turquoise colour but covered with a pattern of enormous pink roses. The skirt was full and long but the bodice plunged down to show a perfectly bronzed back right to the waistline and half of her breasts that were as golden as the nails of her feet encased in strappy turquoise sandals. Sophie tried not to think how shabby she herself must look with her old denim jeans and the girlish checked shirt, and her hair tied back with a blue ribbon.

'Hi, there, Sophie,' Rosine shouted and stopped to speak to Vidal who was still busily laying his bricks. This time however she seemed to be smiling and did not apparently speak as sharply as she had done on the previous encounter with him.

But when she came to Sophie, on the uneven patio, she sank down on to the old deck chair that was all Sophie had to offer her, and looked at her rather scornfully, or so it seemed to Sophie. But this look was soon displaced by a smile that did not somehow ring true.

'What did I tell you? This Vidal is not to be trusted. Always he starts the fights and makes trouble. Just look at his face. I would not wish such a workman to be building on my premises.'

'In this case, Rosine, I don't think it was he who started the fight. According to him some of Fabien's workmen insulted him and egged him on to start fighting.'

Rosine laughed mockingly with the sound of ice tinkling against glass.

'A likely story, when he has the reputation of being one of the fiercest fighters in the district. No one would deliberately start a fight with him.'

'I think they would if they had been urged to do so by someone of higher authority, and also if there were more than two against one.'

'You should not believe everything that a man like Vidal tells you, Sophie. How can you defend him, this man who is nothing better than a peasant and one who constantly makes trouble for everyone?'

'By everyone, I conclude you mean Fabien. As I told you before, Rosine, I am not interested in what Fabien thinks is right. I do not think it right that he is using underhand means to make me sell the *mas* and you can tell him from me he will not succeed by these methods.'

Rosine laughed with a trilling artificial sound.

'You may tell him yourself for I have come to extend to you an invitation to accompany our party to an *aplec* tomorrow. Fabien said you were keen to see the *sardana* danced. Well, here is your opportunity.'

Sophie shook her head.

'I don't think so, Rosine. Are you sure Fabien wanted you to ask me? At the moment I don't feel on such very good terms with *M. le Comte*.'

'Oh, my dear Sophie, don't be like that. You must not miss this opportunity to dance the Sardana. It is going to be a very great occasion for the district and you need hardly speak to Fabien I assure you if you do not wish to. It is to be quite a big party and we are eating at a Catalan restaurant for *déjeuner* before we go to dance. You must not miss this opportunity to see something that is so typical of the Roussillon.'

Why not? thought Sophie. After all, if Rosine was to be there taking up Fabien's attention, he would hardly have time for her, Sophie, and if, as Rosine said, it was to be a large party, they need hardly speak. She did want to see the Sardana. Why should she let the thought of Fabien spoil her enjoyment?

'Very well, Rosine, I'll come. It's true I would like to see an *aplec*. I have never seen a *sardana* danced.'

She wondered what had inspired Rosine to ask her to join the party. Did she want to show her in company that she practically owned Fabien? Had Fabien been consulted about her coming? She thought not and she wondered if he was going to be annoyed by her presence. But she could not worry about that. She offered Rosine coffee but Rosine refused saying that she had to call at the château presently to complete the arrangements with Fabien for tomorrow.

'Fabien relies on me to act as hostess for him,' she informed Sophie. 'Not that he entertains now as he used to do, but all that will change, I promise you, some time in the near future.'

'Why should it change?' asked Sophie, thinking that she well knew the answer.

Rosine laughed lightly. Her lovely face was upturned to the sun and her dark hair shone like a waterfall of pure silk.

'One of these days, Fabien will decide to change his present mode of life, and, when he does, he will need me there. The way he lives now, almost like a monk, is not how he used to live when he was well known in café society. I intend to change all that when . . . but I can't say anything yet.'

'I wouldn't have said he exactly lives like a monk,' said Sophie rather ruefully.

'You wouldn't?' asked Rosine. Her eyes flashed and she looked at Sophie with some suspicion. 'What makes you say that?'

Sophie felt herself blushing. It was as if this other woman could see the evidence of Fabien's kisses on her lips.

'Oh, nothing. Just that he appears attractive to women. I would not have said that was very monk-like.'

Rosine laughed and this time her amusement was genuine.

'Monks are not always unattractive. Haven't you heard of forbidden fruit, Sophie? But how do you know he is attractive to women? Don't you mean one woman, Sophie? Meaning yourself?'

'Not at all, Rosine. Fabien's type has no attractions for me.'

'No?' said Rosine, as if she didn't believe her. 'I think Fabien would attract most women from sixteen to sixty, but, tell me, Sophie, what type of man do you like? I should imagine someone *un peu sérieux, un peu intellectuel* perhaps, not a madman like Fabien. Have you a boyfriend, Sophie, and am I right?'

'Oh, yes, quite right,' Sophie admitted.

She would invent herself a boyfriend, she thought now, of the kind Rosine had described, then Rosine would not suspect her of any interest in Fabien. But why invent one? Her employer, Mike, fitted the bill exactly.

'How clever of you, Rosine. Yes, I have a boyfriend of the *esprit intellectuel* that you describe. His name is Mike Kingsford.'

'Will he be coming here to visit you?' asked Rosine with interest.

'No, not this time. He is tied up with his work and he knows how busy I will be but he phones me constantly.'

'What a pity you can't have him here beside you. You must miss him.'

'Oh, yes, dreadfully,' Sophie told her.

That's true, she thought. She missed his constant nagging to get on with her articles and get started on some other idea he had had; she missed his brilliant, quicksilver brain that was always one jump ahead of her when it came to her work. She felt a pang of guilt. Here she was in France, and she had made Fabien's acquaintance with ease, and still she had hardly started the article she had promised to Mike, and at present it didn't seem as if she would ever get the story from Fabien.

'*Au revoir,*' Rosine shouted, taking off her high-heeled sandals, as she started the yellow car and rushed away. She looked very happy, thought Sophie. Surely she had not come here to find out whether she, Sophie, had any interest in Fabien? But if she had, Sophie had nipped her suspicion in the bud by declaring an interest in Mike Kingsford. Poor Mike. How amused he would be if he knew how she was using his name for this mythical lover, or would he be annoyed? Well, of course, he would never know, thank heaven.

Obviously jeans would not do for the *aplec*. She had been told that everyone joined in. It was a completely communal affair, even though the competitions were danced by experts. She had a white off-the-shoulder gipsy blouse edged with broderie anglaise lace and a full skirt of dark blue cotton banded with a variety of coloured braid. The flowered braid also formed straps in Tyrolean fashion over the blouse, and on her feet she would wear the black espadrilles she had bought at the market in Ceret.

She washed her hair that night in the soft spring water and brushed it until it shone like burnished gold. Vidal and Pujol looked admiringly at her next day when they brought the old truck to the front of the patio. They also had smartened themselves up with their tight black trousers and black waistcoats over white shirts. Their feet were encased in a man's version of the espadrilles so they intended to dance too. They dropped her at the Catalan restaurant that Rosine had named and she was directed to a large circular table full of strangers where she introduced herself and was received very politely. But where were Fabien and Rosine?

'Rosine is always late,' one of the women commented. 'It takes her most of the day to dress and make up.'

'But the result is worth it, *n'est-ce pas?*' said a male member of the party.

'If you think so,' commented his girlfriend with a frown.

'Fabien obviously does,' someone said. 'He is usually an impatient man but not with Rosine.'

'She has him well tamed. Who knows? One of these days quite soon we may expect to dance at their wedding.'

Sophie felt rather a stranger among this crowd of young people who obviously knew each other well. She found it difficult to understand the quick French voices when the conversation was not directed exclusively at her, so, sipping a glass of red wine, she occupied herself in looking around the restaurant.

It had been a Catalan farmhouse with its rough walls and steps and its archways overhead. At one end there was an open fireplace with logs burning and above that was a sloping chimney-breast with pottery plates patterned in primitive design on the mantel. There were strings of onions and garlic hanging from the ceiling and some cured hams, and beside the fireplace stood a spinning-wheel. The seats of the chairs were made of rush and, on a side table, were piled up typical vegetables from this part of the world, yellow and green pumpkins, emerald speckled melons, long yellow squash and green, yellow and red peppers.

The place was crowded as it was a *jour de fête* and there were big family parties at the other tables with many children who seemed to Sophie extraordinarily well behaved.

Heads turned as Fabien and Rosine appeared at the head of the curving stairs. They looked, Sophie thought, a dashingly romantic couple. Fabien was in black knee breeches and white shirt with red cummerbund and white socks with black lacings up the legs. With his dark good looks he could have been a Spanish bullfighter. And Rosine matched him, her full black skirt covered with red roses, her scanty white top showing a great deal of the curves of her breasts, a red hibiscus flower in her hair that was piled up in an elaborate style with a tortoiseshell comb studded with rubies.

'Now at last we can order lunch,' murmured Rosine's neighbour.

'Sorry we are late, my friends,' Rosine declared, not looking in the least repentant.

She was clinging to Fabien as he caressed her arm. Sophie felt a slight tremor shake her. She knew how it felt to have that hand on her body. Never again, she vowed to herself. Fabien did not look surprised to see her. Rosine must have told him she was coming. His smile was just as warm as ever and she found it difficult not to respond in spite of her determination to be cold to him.

After a salad made of olives and artichokes, the main part of the lunch arrived and was set upon the table, a variety of dishes that were, Sophie was told, typical of the Catalan peasant cuisine: rabbit in a savoury sauce, meatballs piled high in their tasty gravy, grilled red peppers with garlic and herbs, cabbage stuffed with ham, mushrooms, garlic, herbs and black olives. This was all accompanied by plenty of wine both white and red but Sophie was careful not to accept more than one glass, and afterwards, for those who had room for it, came a Catalan cream topped with a crackly sweet topping of toffee.

'We'll dance it all down,' the men assured the girls who complained of having eaten too much.

Fabien and Rosine seemed to have gone off on their own and Sophie found herself in a strange car but with very friendly people being driven some miles to an open field where already the sound of music could be heard.

'That's the *cobla* warming up,' she was informed.

There were many people seated casually around the edge of a large field. They had brought seats with them and were apparently chatting with friends and taking not much notice of the music, but Sophie was enchanted with the sweet sharp sound of the *cobla*, which was the band for the *sardana* consisting of strange-looking instruments, the flaviol, a very small piccolo, the tambon, a very small drum the size of a teacup that was fixed to the flaviol player's elbow, and there was also a kind of euphonium and a double bass.

'When are they going to start?' asked Sophie impatiently of her neighbour. 'Nobody seems to be the least interested in the music.'

'Soon the dance will begin. It looks simple but it is really quite intricate, *très mathématique*. It is almost a sacred dance here, you know, a dance symbolising peace and brotherhood.'

Suddenly it seemed the crowd recognised a signal to start dancing. First one, then two, then more circles were formed with everyone laughing and joining hands. Sophie hung back wanting to watch before she ventured to join in but the others formed their own large laughing circle. At first the music was slow and feet in black espadrilles took up the rhythm, then faster and everything became lively with the crowds springing up and down to the sweet sharp sounds of the *cobla*. The more professional-looking dancers were dressed in colourful dresses with black aprons and black shawls, white stockings and espadrilles with criss-crossed braiding on the legs. But everyone joined in, from grandparents to the tiniest toddler. Those who had at first hesitated were carried away by the music as if under the spell of the Pied Piper, and drifted towards the rings where the dancers willingly made room for them. Sophie longed to dance but hesitated to, afraid she would not be able to manage the intricate rhythm of the *sardana*.

'Come, Sophie, we'll practise the steps together.'

She looked up startled and there was Fabien, who had broken away from the circle and come to stand beside her. She saw Rosine give a displeased glance behind her but there was nothing she could do, for the rhythm had just changed to a lilting, bouncing note and everyone else was dancing furiously to keep up with the music.

Fabien led her to a quiet corner and there proceeded to instruct her in the timing of the steps she must follow. It seemed easy when she did it with him, but every now and again she lost the step and sighed with exasperation.

'If all those grannies and little children can do it, I should be able to,' she moaned.

She had forgotten her exasperation with Fabien as he taught her to dance, smiling down at her with all his charm. How was it that by just being with him, she could be persuaded to forget all his shortcomings? She had vowed to forget the effect of his touch upon her and yet here she was holding his hand as he seriously taught her the steps of the *sardana* and she felt carried away by the joyousness of the music and the fact that she was with him again and he no longer seemed to be an enemy. Perhaps after all Vidal had been partly to blame for that fight.

Yet when Fabien made as if to kiss her at the end of his instructions, she shied away from him and, not making any comment but shrugging his shoulders, he led her back to the dance. Now she felt more confident as Fabien broke the circle and, holding her hand, counted for her as she took up the rhythm. She had to concentrate hard so did not notice at first that Rosine had left the dancing. It was such a lovely feeling to be joining in the dance with all these other people. A great laughing crowd, all looking extremely happy, concentrating on this strange, sweet music with its exacting rhythms, first slow then fast. The announcements were in the Catalan language but Sophie did not mind that she could not understand. It was enough to be dancing here under the warm sun in such pleasant company, feeling Fabien's hand in hers and hearing his instructions and his laughter when she missed a step.

At the end of the dance, Fabien led her back to where the crowd of friends were seated and it was then that Sophie noticed Rosine had fastened her attentions on to Pierre, the young man who had told Sophie about the *sardana* when they had first arrived. Her back was very obviously turned away from Fabien and Sophie, and she was caressing Pierre, her hands smoothing his handsome face. He caught her hand and kissed it then stole a guilty look in Fabien's direction. Rosine was being deliberately provocative, thought Sophie. She was probably furious that Fabien had left her to give instructions to Sophie, but, if indeed she was trying to provoke him, *M. le Comte* was ignoring it. Or was he? He began to talk most charmingly to Sophie and pointed out things of interest about the *aplec*, meanwhile putting his arm around her shoulders to show her the objects he meant, the instruments of the band, the people of importance famous for their proficiency in the dance. This, thought Sophie, was all done to annoy Rosine. What a pair they made, both equally arrogant and self-willed!

'I must go to look for Vidal. It's time I went home,' Sophie told him.

She was determined not to be used to make Rosine jealous.

'Vidal? Surely you aren't going to take a lift from him? By now I should think he is too drunk to drive. It will be wiser if you let him sleep it off and come back to work in the morning, if, of course, he has recovered by that time, which I doubt.'

'You have a very low opinion of him, don't you? All the same I'm going to look for him.'

Fabien shrugged.

'If you insist on it, I'd better come with you. The bar isn't a fit place for a woman to visit alone.'

'Oh, don't be so mediaeval,' cried Sophie impatiently, but Fabien came with her across the field to where there was a kind of open-air bar set up. There was no sign of Vidal but suddenly Pujol appeared in front of them seemingly in great distress. He had some kind of impediment in his speech and Sophie would have found it very difficult to understand him without Fabien's help.

His clothes were torn and his face grazed as if he had been fighting and so it proved.

'He says your precious Vidal has landed in prison,' Fabien informed her. 'Together with two of my workmen. It seems they were arrested for fighting here.'

'Oh, not again,' groaned Sophie.

'What do you mean, not again?' Fabien demanded.

'Your men deliberately goaded Vidal in Ceret so that he got involved in a fight there. I thought you knew.'

'How would I have known?'

'They insulted him because he was working for a woman and a foreigner.'

'And you thought I had encouraged this. What a poor opinion you have of me, Sophie.'

'If I have it is your own fault,' Sophie cried.

'Anyway Vidal does not need much encouragement to join in a fight. I warned you before you should never have employed him.'

'And who else could I employ?' Sophie asked. 'You had already taken all the workmen in the village deliberately to frustrate me. Vidal suits me well enough if your workmen will leave him alone.'

'Well, I guess we'll have to go and bail them out,' Fabien said.

When they reached the prison, it appeared that Fabien for once was right and that Vidal was not entirely innocent. It was he who had picked a fight with the workmen who had previously attacked him.

'What is it you English say, six of one and half a dozen of the other,' said Fabien. 'I have arranged to pay their fines but meanwhile I have advised the *gardien* of the prison that he should let them cool their heels overnight.'

'You are so high-handed,' Sophie protested. 'You always think you know what's best for people, don't you? Now how am I going to get home?'

'We'll fix something,' Fabien told her.

Rosine would be less than delighted if she was to accompany them, thought Sophie. She would have to get a lift with one of the others, all strangers to her, and most of them living in another direction. When they arrived back at the *aplec*, the group of friends seemed to be breaking up and Rosine was nowhere to be seen. Several women seemed to take a delight in informing Fabien that she had gone off with Pierre. A look of annoyance flashed across his face but he quickly seemed to recover.

'That has worked out well,' he told Sophie. 'Now I am free to take you home.'

Sophie told herself she did not really want to go home with Fabien, but all the same, as she sat in the silver sports-car and was driven away from the *aplec*, she felt a thrill of pure happiness. It had been such a glorious day.

She glanced at Fabien's dark profile. How difficult it was to know what he was thinking. Obviously he had been annoyed by Rosine's desertion but he had immediately hidden it from the others, who had looked at him curiously, wondering how he would react. They had also been looking at her in an odd way, wondering whether Fabien was taking too much interest in his foreign neighbour. Rosine had probably been furious because he had accompanied her to the prison, and she was not one to hide her feelings. She had gone off with Pierre doubtless to teach Fabien a lesson, but Fabien did not appear very teachable in these matters. He was a difficult man to cross.

She leaned back in her seat enjoying the cooler air streaming towards her and enjoying the scenery so different from that of England, the vines climbing up the sandy-looking hillsides, the cherry orchards in the sun-scorched valleys, and the rusty gold of the little farmhouses shining now in the late afternoon sunshine under their roofs of rose-coloured tiles.

They seemed to be taking a different route from that they had followed in the morning and she commented on this.

'I've decided you should see some more of the country,' Fabien said. 'We shouldn't miss the opportunity. Today is a *jour de fête* and you have lost Vidal so you cannot go home to work on the *mas*. Therefore I have decided you should go up the mountain with me. There's still plenty of daylight left.'

'And how do you know I want to go up the mountain with you?' Sophie demanded. 'You didn't even ask me.'

'I know you will enjoy this part of our lovely countryside, my dear Sophie.'

And with that she had to be content. She had not intended to have any more to do with Fabien and yet here she was practically being kidnapped and taken to some strange place just because he wanted to show that Rosine's defection had meant nothing to him. He was using her again just to get his own back on Rosine. But there was not much she could do about it, short of jumping out of the car that was now executing sweeping swerves around hairpin bends as they drove further and further up the mountain road.

Below them were deep gorges and thick forests and sometimes there were high bridges that they seemed to hurtle across. Above them pink rocks seemed to rise over the dark trees.

'Where are you taking me?' asked Sophie, clinging to the side of her seat.

Fabian took one hand from the wheel and patted her knee reassuringly but Sophie longed for him to concentrate on the winding road.

'You shall see when we get to the top, and, I promise you, you are going to enjoy it.'

CHAPTER SEVEN

'THESE mountains form the border between France and Spain,' Fabien informed her.

It seemed to Sophie that they had been driving for ever up the winding road with high wooded slopes on one side and vistas of wild country below. They met no other cars, no other people. It seemed they were the only people left in the world. But now they arrived at a place where the woods on one side came up to the road and paths could be seen leading through the forest. On the other side, perched high above the stupendous view, was a chalet made of wood which was a restaurant for travellers.

'Just a moment while I make arrangements here, Sophie. We'll dine here later.'

He didn't ask her whether she wanted to dine with him, thought Sophie, and then another thought struck her. There was a sign reading, '*Chambres à louer*,'—rooms to let. Now that he had kidnapped her, did he intend they should spend the night together? If so he was going to be sadly disappointed.

He came out looking cheerful and climbed back into the car.

'We'll go to the highest point, where we can see into Spain,' he told her.

They drove on and now the forest fell away and the slopes were sun-scorched and covered with tiny heath-like plants, scrub that had a pungent fragrance of something like thyme, borne to them on the stiff breeze. Fabien helped Sophie out of the car and they went through a fence on to the rugged slopes.

'Now you are in Spain,' he told her.

The wind was very strong and, although she had vowed she would avoid his touch, she was glad of the support of his

arm around her waist as she swayed in the teeth of the gale.
Around them, where they had trodden, rose the fragrance
of thyme and, far below as if it were in another world, there
was the plain criss-crossed with roads joining small towns
with white houses and stone churches.

She felt his hand on her chin turning her face towards
him and then she was lost in the passion of his kiss, the
curves of her body pressed against the hardness of his. She
could not tell whether the throbbing beat she could sense
was from his heart or her own, so closely was she part of
him. And all the time the wind was tugging at her
streaming hair, threatening to tear her away so that, in
spite of her doubts, Fabien seemed to be her refuge from the
elements. For now, as he released her, she saw that the scene
had changed. The wild wind had brought up billowing
clouds upon the mountain. Below them the green pastures
had become blue and, where they were still in sunlight,
they were covered by the shadows of hurrying clouds.

'Is there going to be a storm?' she asked.

He shrugged his shoulders.

'The weather can change very quickly here in these high
regions, but it will probably pass just as swiftly. Don't
worry, Sophie. I know this country. You are quite safe with
me.'

That is the last thing that she could be sure of, thought
Sophie. Should she insist on being taken back down the
mountain right now? It was true that he knew the
mountain weather and possibly the storm would pass and
they would have a beautiful evening. But she would have to
be careful. At the back of her mind she knew very well that
this excursion with her had only been caused by the fact
that Rosine had gone off with someone else, so she must
remember only that and forget the emotion aroused in her
body by that passionate, lingering kiss. He was using her for
his own purposes as he had done all along.

As they came into the chalet, the wind was still howling
all around them and mists had obscured the tops of the
higher mountains. The building seemed to shake with the

force of the gale but the walls were of sturdy pinewood
although it stood upon stilts high above the panorama of
mountain scenery. The *propriétaire* came hurrying towards
them, a woman in one of those dark flowered aprons that
Sophie had seen hanging in racks at the Ceret market, her
hair in rollers.

'*Enchantée, monsieur et madame, comment ça va? Quel orage!*'

She produced hot tisane and apple pie beautifully
arranged in sliced concentric circles. There was a group of
young people who had also come in to shelter from the
storm and Sophie felt glad of their presence for she had not
wanted to be alone with Fabien. She wanted to dismiss the
dark intensity of his expression, to forget that the woman
who owned the chalet had called her Madame.

By now thunder was rolling around the mountains and
lightning flashing among the high peaks, but still the rain
held off, though black clouds had begun to gather and the
sun had disappeared.

The young crowd at first had appeared very bright and
happy, teasing each other and laughing and joking while
they ate apple pie and drank their tins of Coke or lager. But
soon, as the storm of wind and thunder raged on, they
appeared to become uneasy. It seemed three of their
number were missing. Now the threatened rain had started
in earnest, drumming on the roof with tropical intensity,
and the vast panorama of valley and mountain was blotted
out as if a curtain had been lowered.

Suddenly there was a drumming of feet on the open deck
outside and the door was flung open. A young girl
staggered into the room, her clothing soaked, her hair
streaming with water.

'*Au secours,*' she gasped.

From the frantic conversation that followed, Sophie
gathered that she and two young men had tried to climb
down one of the cliffs below the chalet and that one young
man had panicked and was now stuck half-way, not able to
move up or down and glued against the rock face with a
drop of hundreds of feet into the valley below. The two

others had been trying to persuade him to move, but now the storm had arrived and his position was even more desperate. The crowd of young people were like a flock of frightened birds as they hovered about bewildered and not knowing what to do.

Sophie realised that, under the bronze of his skin, Fabien had gone pale. His face had a greyish tinge and his eyes were the dark colour of polished onyx, but he arose from his seat and spoke to the panicking teenagers.

'We'll have to act fast. There's no time to lose.'

He turned to the half-drowned-looking girl.

'You, show me where this has happened. Hurry now. And stop weeping. That won't help at all. And, Sophie, go and ask Madame for a rope and bring it after me.'

Before Sophie could say a word, he had gone out into the storm with the frightened youngsters. Sophie went to demand a rope from Madame, who, much to her relief, produced a sturdy one, then she too hurried out into the rain. Fortunately in spite of the bad conditions, she could still see some of the youngsters straggling behind as if not wanting to face what lay ahead, and she herself hurried past them feeling horribly scared but aiming to get to Fabien and help him however she could.

She was in time to see him on the top of the cliff where the land fell away precipitously into the valley. He was taking off his black jacket and the espadrilles he had worn to the *aplec.*

'Oh, Sophie, good, you have brought the rope,' he said very casually. 'I'll tie it to this rock and use it if need be to hoist our friend up. I myself will climb down. It isn't very far.'

Sophie braced herself to look below over the cliff. About thirty metres down she could see a figure spread-eagled upon the rocks and a little way underneath him there was a tiny ledge. Beyond that there was a drop of hundreds of metres into the valley below where rocks thrust up jagged teeth.

'How can you?' Sophie asked. 'You haven't even got any

shoes or proper equipment.'

Fabien laughed. He was still pale and his eyes glittered with a strange expression.

'*Cela ne fait rien.* It will not be the first time that I have had to climb barefoot. You would not wish me to leave this boy there to fall to his death on those rocks below?'

'Can't we get someone who is familiar with the place? Isn't there a warden or a mountain rescue service we could summon?'

'I've no time to argue, Sophie. It would take far too long to get help. Can't you see that the boy has only a little while before he loses his grip? Now hold on to this rope and see that the others let it out carefully. Don't look so worried. I've been in far worse situations than this.'

All the same Sophie was desperately frightened for him for she could see that, in spite of his seeming courage, his hands were trembling and his face had lost all the lovely warm colour that normally flushed the gold of his cheeks. Knowing something of his previous history, she wondered whether that tragedy on the Eiger had made him lose his nerve, and, if it had, how could he rescue this boy high above the valley and those jagged rocks?

He took the end of the rope in his hands and she watched as he disappeared over the edge of the cliff. The climb down was slow and she watched anxiously, expecting that with his bare feet he might slip. The teenagers were chattering like jays and she abruptly told them to be quiet, but in the hush that followed it seemed even worse to see that laborious slow progress down the face of the cliff. But he was getting there. Once he looked up at her and she could see that his face was grey and his expression grim, but he tried to smile, even raised one hand and gave her a little wave.

'Oh, please don't do that,' she shouted. 'Hold on with both hands.'

He was now right near the frightened boy but he went past him until he stood on the small ledge below. Then he started to speak. Sophie could not hear what he was saying but his tone was low and persuasive. The young people were all silent now, some with their heads over the edge, but some of the girls were obviously unable to look.

It seemed hours to Sophie before she saw the boy's arms and then his feet move. The crowd clustered above gave an exclamation of appreciation, quickly hushed. Slowly and painfully the boy came down to the ledge where Fabien was standing. There was barely room for the two of them there, but Fabien put the rope around the boy's waist and gave the signal to hoist him up from there. There were many hands to make light work of the task of getting him up and the girls were in tears as his body came up over the edge of the cliff, scraped and scratched but otherwise unharmed.

Already Fabien had started the climb back. Only Sophie watched him. The others were totally concerned with their own friend. Why, she wondered, hadn't he waited for the rope to be let down again? But she supposed he would be too proud of his climbing skill to let himself be hauled up in that ignominious fashion.

Her breath caught once as he appeared to slip, but he held on and slowly, very slowly edged up towards the top. She felt she could not bear to watch his slow progress and yet she could not look away. If he were to fall now . . . that strong active body, that body that seemed made for thrills and excitement could lie broken and bleeding on the teeth of those black rocks beneath the cliff. If he were to be killed, she thought, I could not bear it. How could he risk his life for a careless teenager? For the young people, now that their friend was safe, seemed to be taking no more interest in the proceedings. They were laughing and joking among themselves, and the drama of the rescue had already been forgotten. Don't you know, she wanted to shout at them, that a man is still climbing up this dangerous cliff that is slippery with rain and that at any moment he could fall to his death?

'Help me to get him over the top,' she implored two of them and they gave exclamations of surprise as if they were astonished that Fabien was still battling his way up.

But he needed no help. He hauled his body, drenched and scratched, over the edge and lay exhausted on the muddy ground.

'Are you all right?' Sophie exclaimed.

She bent over him and he put his hand out to touch her face.

'Why are you weeping, Sophie?' he asked.

Hastily she brushed the tears from her face.

'I'm not. That's the rain,' she told him.

He, who despised tears, was not going to have the satisfaction of knowing he had made her cry.

'Why did you do it?' she demanded. 'Look at them. They are not even grateful. They just took it all for granted that you risked your life.'

He laughed and it seemed that some of his vigour was returning to him.

'Don't make such a big drama of it, Sophie. There was little danger to me and I don't want gratitude. *Cela ne fait rien.* Hauling up a frightened teenager was not a big affair, not a matter for your Victoria Cross or the Croix de Guerre.'

But as they made their way slowly back to the chalet, he held fast to her waist and she noticed that his limp seemed worse. By the time they had reached there, the young people had gone. They could hear the sound of their motor-bikes roaring down the curving roads as they went at speed clad in jeans and black leather jackets, the girls clinging on to the drivers on their pillion seats.

Madame, minus her curlers now and in an elaborate flowered dress, greeted them with concern.

'Oh, *monsieur et madame*, how glad I am to see you safely back, but look how you are soaked. I will find you clothes and put your own near to the stove. You cannot stay like that. You must be dry to eat the meal I have cooked for you.'

Sophie had thought they should commence the journey down the mountain before the weather worsened, but

obviously now Fabien needed to rest awhile and Madame
had already cooked the meal. Now very apologetically she
produced some faded garments that looked as if they had
come from some bygone age, as indeed they had.

'My late mother's best dress,' she told them. 'She wore it
very seldom. In fact she was married in it and wore it on her
feast days, but it is very clean and has been in a chest for
many years. And for you, monsieur, my father's suit. This
also was hardly worn and he was buried in his second-best
garment.'

The dress was very pretty, made of sprigged lilac cotton
with a tight bodice high to the neck buttoning with many
tiny pearl buttons and a kind of bustle at the back of the
skirt.

'You look perfectly charming in that,' said Fabien, when
they had both changed.

She had not been able to fasten all the buttons but had
folded back the bodice in a rather décolleté fashion. He too,
looked imposing in the strictly formal black trousers and
jacket with white shirt. The clothes were a little too tight
and emphasised his slim muscular legs and the broad
shoulders and strong muscles of his chest.

'And now I think we really deserve an aperitif,' he said.
'You shall have some Rancio which is made in the
Roussillon and I will have a whisky if Madame can
produce one. I don't normally drink spirits when I am
going to have wine with a meal but tonight I feel I need one,
maybe even a double.'

He had recovered his healthy colouring now and she felt
glad, for she had been worried by that grey, haggard look
as she had gazed down at him on the mountain with the
horrible space below him. He was perhaps quieter than
usual and she realised that she felt concerned about him.
She had forgotten her feelings of hostility, forgotten that
she had believed he had brought her here because he
wanted to have his revenge on Rosine for going off with
that other man. She had seen him risk his life for someone
whose name they didn't even know, someone who had not

even stayed to thank him. Whatever had happened in the past, there was no doubt about his courage, and she would be able to say that when she wrote that article about him.

The article? Perhaps the time had come now when she could find out more about him, and yet she felt unwilling to try. With the warm glow of the aperitif flowing through her veins, she felt relaxed and content just to be here with him, alive and vibrantly handsome, so different from what might have been. She would enjoy his company this evening and not think of their differences. But if he had ideas of making love to her up here in this mountain retreat, what then?

For a first course, Madame gave them a piperade, a mixture of sweet peppers, tomatoes and onions with eggs added at the last minute to give a scrambled effect. As she was cooking, the appetising smell of hot olive oil penetrated into the dining-room from the kitchen. With this she served thin slices of smoked meat from the ham that was hanging from a hook. Next she served partridges cooked in the Catalan manner in a white wine, the Rancio wine of the Roussillon, with a small glass of port added, together with sweet red peppers, garlic and Seville oranges and black olives.

'Madame has rather overdone the peppers perhaps,' said Fabien. 'But they are favourites in the Catalan style of cooking.'

'It is all delicious,' Sophie told him.

She felt tremendously hungry and somehow very happy.

'The mountain air has been good for you in spite of the storm,' Fabien told her. 'Those blue eyes are like sapphires and your hair is like fire.'

'I had better not eat too much in case I split *Grand'mère's* gown,' she laughed.

She had forgotten about the storm and yet the rain was still battering against the windows and the thunder rolling around the peaks. It was quite dark now and she wondered how they were to get home but she dismissed the thought. It was enough to be here with Fabien vividly alive across the table from her, his dark eyes admiring her, instead of lying at the bottom of the valley, broken and shattered, and when he refilled her glass she did not refuse. The golden wine, the good food, and his gaze that was on her all the time, made her forget that outside there was a world of storm and that soon they would have to venture out into the night in the small silver sports-car and make their way down the windswept mountain into the everyday world.

But Madame came bustling in with some more garments, a nightshirt for Fabien and a voluminous nightdress for Sophie, trimmed with lace and most beautifully embroidered.

'I have prepared a room for you,' she announced. 'There are two beds if you wish it, but I would recommend the right one, Monsieur. It is much more comfortable.'

'But I thought . . .' protested Sophie.

She did not like to make a fuss in front of Madame who seemed so eager to please.

But as soon as she had gone she turned furiously to Fabien.

'How could you? You didn't even ask me if I were willing to stay.'

Fabien took her hand and smoothed her arm, as if, thought Sophie indignantly, he were soothing a restless pony.

'You have no choice, Sophie. Madame told me a little while ago that the bridge is down over the river below. There is no way to get across until it can be fixed by daylight. She has only one room here, but as you heard her say there are two beds. It is up to you what you choose to do. Whatever happens we are here for the night and we must make the best of it, *n'est-ce pas?*'

'I think that your idea of making the best of it differs somewhat from mine,' Sophie declared.

'Oh, my Sophie,' said Fabien with his most engaging smile. 'What a bad opinion you always persist in having of me. You should know that nothing can happen to you against your wishes.'

That is what she was afraid of, thought Sophie,

remembering the sensations that had swept over her when Fabien had kissed her on the mountain. And feeling as she did after he had risked his life, she wondered if she could still refuse him.

'But there is no hurry, Sophie. If Madame could produce a brandy, I think it might do us both good.'

Madame brought a pot of coffee together with a bottle of Courvoisier and then she bade them goodnight. The electricity had failed during the storm and they were left with the glow of a candle stuck in an old wine-bottle.

'You look even lovelier by this golden light,' Fabien declared, reaching across the table to take her hand. 'Dear Sophie, how sweet you were when you thought I was in danger. I won't easily forget the alarm in those huge frightened blue eyes as you looked over the cliff.'

'Only *thought* you were in danger?' Sophie told him crossly. 'You were in danger. You could have lost your life.'

'No, Sophie, it was not such a heroic thing that I did. You must not exaggerate. Scrambling down a rock face to save a terrified teenager. *Cela ne fait rien.* It was nothing. If only it had been as easy that other time, then my life could have been different altogether.'

'What other time was that?' Sophie asked quietly.

Fabien got up to put another log on the fire and poured himself some more brandy.

'That time on the Eiger. It is some years ago now. Ah, but you do not know, do you? I was a climber and I had had a certain amount of publicity for it. Too much, perhaps. The one climb that had eluded me was the famous North Face of the Eiger. I had made one or two attempts but always I had been driven back by bad weather. It's a particularly gruelling rock face. Even the name means the Ogre. It has faced every storm in Europe for thousands of years and the rocks are not hard but often weak and crumbling, nor can the weather on the face be relied upon for more than half a day at a time. I had arranged to climb it with three friends, Armand, Jerome and Emile. We had accomplished many climbs together and we had been waiting at Kleine

Scheidegg for the weather to clear.

'At that time, I was a different character from the man I am now. I was younger and carefree, careless perhaps. The waiting bored me and, the way I was used to living, I couldn't stand to be bored. There was a girl staying at the hotel, a beautiful blonde. I started a quick, passionate affair with her, a thing of the body only. I was drinking too much. I always prided myself that drink did not affect me. We have been waiting so long for the day we could climb that I began to believe it would never come. Although the Met men told us the weather might have cleared by the next day, I only half believed it and, since the blonde and I had been asked to a hectic party, I was determined not to miss it. So, when the next day came and the weather was clear, there was I suffering from the grandfather of a hangover and I had expended much physical energy in other ways, I assure you. I suppose I wasn't really fit to climb but nobody dared tell me. In any case I would have taken not a bit of notice even if they had.

'In spite of all this, the climb went well to start with. We climbed on two ropes and made good progress. We had taken plenty of food and good bivouac equipment, and that night we settled down on a ledge keeping warm together in two small tents. Perhaps the amount I had taken to drink the night before had made me careless. Anyhow it was I who dropped the rucksack containing the food over the edge. It rolled away down the mountain to the rocks hundreds of feet below. That was a blow, I can tell you, but worse was to follow. The wind got up, followed by a blizzard. There we were, hundreds of feet up with no food and a storm brewing. Next day conditions were a little improved and we set out determined to reach the top whatever happened.

'Armand was feeling ill, but insisted on continuing. We all felt a little weak, I think, from lack of food, and became a little light-headed. We went on but this time the climbing was more difficult and we moved very slowly. Then Armand slipped and fell while moving over a tricky traverse at the end of the rope. He was injured but still conscious and he managed to rope himself to a narrow ledge on the face. We could do nothing to get him then but shouted down to him that we would organise his rescue as soon as we could. The weather now had become worse and the whole face was covered with swirling mist but still we were determined to go on. I think by this time we were not quite sane. We should have gone down then while we still could and asked for people who could help Armand, but we went on.

'Jerome was the next to go. He was leading at the time and a rock came from up above and hit him on the head. It was obvious to us then, mad as we were, that he could not continue, and we put up a tent for him and left him there. Emile and I pressed on. It was getting hard to breathe in the thin air and the swirling snow, and yet we laughed and sang old songs from our days in the army as conscripts. As I said before we were *un peu fou*, a little mad.

'I was doing the leading now and I felt in spite of all our setbacks that this time we were really going to reach the top. I hammered a piton into the rock and Emile belayed himself to the rope, then I climbed up across the overhang and stood on the ledge and stretched. I was not watching the rope. I was looking towards the summit and realising with terrific excitement that we had nearly made it. We were almost there. Then I heard a shout. Even today when the years have passed, that scream haunts my dreams. The piton, that piton that I had hammered into the rock had come out. As I said before the rock on the face can be very bad, very crumbling. With the sudden jerk, the rope had grazed against a sharp rock and was cut. I saw Emile's body hurtling hundreds of feet, turning over and over to fall on the rocks somewhere far below.

'And I went on. Can you believe it? I went on. In my mind there was only one idea, to conquer that face that had brought us so much misfortune. I should have gone back, turned back before it was too late for the others but I went on and I got to the summit. I stood on the top of that

mountain and shook my fist at God and it was then that I
came to my senses and realised what I had done. I had left
my friends injured and suffering and one of them dead just
so that I could say I had climbed the North Face.

'I came down by another route but, as I descended, when
I got to the spot where we had left Armand, I could hear
him calling, a desperate cry for help. And then I too fell,
only a little way down the mountain but enough to injure a
leg. Even when I was trying to help, I was careless. If I had
been more careful, it might not have been too late.

'I managed to get myself to the railway, the one that goes
down from the Jungfraujoch. There are openings in the
tunnel and I found one and made my way down to Kleine
Scheidegg. They called out the mountain rescue team and I
went back with them and showed them where to go, but it
was all in vain. Armand with no tent and just on a ledge
had been swept off by the blizzard and was hanging frozen
on the end of his rope. Jerome had died from his injuries
and the cold, and Emile, well, they never found his body.
Only I survived, I and my pride. I had conquered the North
Face but at the cost of my self-respect. So now you know the
story, something I have never confided to anyone before
now.'

Sophie looked at Fabien. His hands were trembling as he
poured himself some more brandy and his eyes were the
colour of dark wine. While he had been telling her the
story, she had lived it with him, but now she leaned across
and took his hand in hers.

'But, Fabien, don't you think your friends would have
wanted you to continue? It would have made their
sufferings seem more worth while if they could have known
you conquered the wall. You owed it to them to finish the
climb.'

'You are very sweet, Sophie, trying so hard to make it
right, but for years I have lived with this feeling that I
should in some way have been able to save them.'

'But that's foolish, Fabien, you can't make over the past. I
know the history of the North Face of the Eiger and how

difficult it is and how many good climbers have been lost there. You were young and perhaps too daring but the other three took an equal chance. You could not hold yourself responsible for everything that happened to them. There must have been other weaknesses. You can't put it all down to your own fault.'

'For years I have lived with the idea that I lacked courage.'

'Oh, Fabien, how can you say that? With an injured leg, you struggled down the mountain and, when you got there, you did not think of leaving it to the others to rescue your friends but went back with them injured as you were. As for that piton, you said yourself the rocks are centuries old and crumbling. You could not have known that that particular rock would fail you. I saw this evening how courageous you were. You did not give a thought to the fact that you were in great danger. Even now you won't admit you were.'

Fabien gave a great sigh and touched her face with his hand.

'Bless you, Sophie, for trying to lift away some of my guilt, but the only way I can ever regain my pride in myself is if I do something outstandingly courageous, something where I have no thought for myself but only for the other person, the one who is in peril.'

'But, good heavens, Fabien, didn't you do that tonight?'

'Not really, Sophie. As I told you, it was a simple thing for a seasoned mountaineer to do and yet, as no doubt you could see, I lacked courage even there. My hands trembled and my heart beat fast. No, Sophie, I need to do something that cancels out the past. I had thought the episode this evening might be the one, but then I found that, even in that small adventure, my nerves were breaking.'

'But that's absurd, Fabien. No one could have shown more courage than you did in rescuing that ungrateful teenager.'

He laughed and shook his head.

'Let's change the subject, Sophie. We have talked about me long enough. You need to rest now. You have had a long day. Go and try Madame's best nightdress for size. As for me, I'll stay by the fire. Talking of the past has brought it all back to me. I have much to think about.'

It was not the end to the evening that she had imagined, and yet she was glad of it. After this serious talk with Fabien, she felt as if all her defences were down. Underneath all that arrogance there existed a large area of self-doubt, and that was why he had withdrawn from his previous mode of life. And yet her own arguments had been heartfelt. He seemed to her the most courageous man she had ever known. She had thought they were enemies but now against her will she found herself admiring him. She had known from the first that he possessed enormous physical attraction, but now reluctantly she realised that she could feel fondness for him if she allowed herself to do so.

Some time during the night she awoke to the awareness that he had come into the room and was lying fully clothed upon the other bed. As she stirred, he came across to her and touched her hair. Kneeling beside her, he began to kiss her gently. She put her arms around him and drew him down towards her. For a long time it seemed to her she was becoming lost in sensation, reaching towards something more heavenly than she had ever known. But suddenly he drew back, stood up and strode away from the bed. She saw his broad shoulders outlined against the lighter dark of the unshuttered windows.

'I cannot take your surrender, Sophie, simply because you feel sorry for me. No woman has accepted me simply out of pity and it is not going to happen now. One day soon maybe you will feel passion for me, then that will be a different story.'

Sophie longed to say that it was passion she felt now but something made her hold back. This whole episode up on the mountain had to her seemed like a dream. In her present mood she wanted to go on dreaming, but how would she feel when she at last awoke?

CHAPTER EIGHT

'PENANCE after confession,' Fabien declared as they drove
in sunlight down the mountainside. 'Tomorrow I intend to
take you to Saint Martin, where we will have to walk up to
the monastery on our own two feet. But I promise you that,
once we get there, you will see some glorious views as well
as exquisite Romanesque sculpture.'

'But I mustn't waste any more time on sightseeing,'
Sophie protested. 'My time here is very limited.'

'You consider yesterday a waste of time?' asked Fabien.
'If so, it was a very delightful way to do so.'

He was laughing again and he had that wicked,
mischievous smile on his lips. Was it a dream that she had
been so willing to have him make love to her? She had been
saved not by her own will but by his restraint. They were
driving down the mountain and the bridge had been
repaired. All around them there were signs of the storm,
trees down, waterfalls cascading down the cliffs in veils of
white lace, but the sun was shining balmy and warm,
making the steam rise from the shining grass.

By the time they came back to the *mas*, Vidal had already
arrived and was working with Pujol upon the roof. He was
totally unrepentant about his fight and did not look very
much the worse for wear.

'The others are nursing sore heads,' he told Sophie. 'They
won't mock me again.'

Fabien had left her at the end of the drive but she
wondered whether Vidal had seen the silver car flashing
through the trees. If so, he was too discreet to comment.
Fabien had kissed her when they parted, a gentle kiss with
only a promise of the passion she had experienced before.

'I'll call for you tomorrow,' he promised. 'Bernadette will
pack a picnic basket for us. The weather looks good. No

more storms, and yet I felt that storm was sent from heaven especially for us.'

That morning she left the garden work alone, feeling deliciously lazy, but she brought her typewriter on to the patio and sat in the shade occasionally writing a sentence but most of the time lost in a dream. She thought it was absurd of her to be feeling so happy and yet she could not help it. Nothing had changed. Presumably Fabien still wanted to buy the *mas* and Rosine still had first claim on him. The problem of Fabien remained in spite of the fact that yesterday she had learned so much more about him. But she would not write that article, not now. She felt it would be a breach of confidence if she did so.

Yet all the same it had always been her custom to write down her own impressions after some event that had completely caught her interest, so she looked at her previous notes on Fabien and proceeded to add to them. She wrote about his character and then she wrote his story, adding her own reflections on the reasons he felt so much guilt, and her own ideas about this.

When she had finished, she felt calm and peaceful as if she had accomplished something splendid. It would never appear in print now, but it was an intimate profile of a man who, in spite of all his faults, she could not help admiring. Was it more than admiration? No, no, she could not admit such a thought. Last night she had forgotten about Rosine, but today she must forget those passionate emotions that had arisen when Fabien embraced her.

Now Vidal interrupted her thoughts.

'*Mademoiselle Rouquine*, soon I will be needing more materials. The work is going well and I'll need more tiles for the roof and the inside floors.'

She must bestir herself from her dreaming and work out her finances. Mike would be furious that she had decided not to go ahead with the article on Fabien but she could not do it now. What else could she write about to earn some money? It was difficult to think of anything because here she could have no thoughts except those that concerned either the *mas* or Fabien. She wondered again what had happened to the pictures. If only she could find them her financial problems could be solved.

She put aside her writing and proceeded to try to work out her accounts, and she was alarmed and distressed to find that she had less money left than she had thought. If she didn't get some money from somewhere, she would have to call a halt to the repairs. Vidal was working for very little but all the materials were costly and soon they would need some more. Perhaps Mike would let her borrow on her salary, but she felt doubtful because he was going to be displeased that she had not progressed with the proposed article.

But she couldn't send it to him now, that intimate portrait of Fabien. He had told her a story he had never confided to anyone before. She supposed it was a journalist's dream of a scoop, but even her lack of funds couldn't persuade her to send the story to be printed. She would have to think of some other way.

That evening she had a visit from Rosine. She came clattering over the rough stones of the patio in her usual high-heeled sandals, wearing a tight tube of white twisted material over her breasts and red linen culottes.

'Hi, Sophie,' she cried. 'Did you miss me yesterday? I decided to go home with Pierre. I found the *aplec* so boring. It's too terribly rustic, don't you think?'

'I thought it was interesting,' Sophie told her.

'I don't find it so,' said Rosine. 'It's supposed to be an event of peace and love, but your workman Vidal doesn't seem to have heard of that. Wasn't it fortunate that Fabien was able to deal with that little episode? But of course Fabien is always marvellous at managing people.'

'So I've noticed,' Sophie told her drily.

'I didn't realise that you two had gone to the prison. Otherwise I might not have gone off with Pierre. Fabien is so frantically jealous if I look at another man, but I went to him and we made it up this afternoon. It is easy to manage a

man, even a man like Fabien, if you use the right
technique.'

Sophie was surprised by the wave of wild rage that she
felt sweep over her. She was back again where she had
started, she thought, enraged and irritated by both Rosine
and Fabien. At least Rosine seemed unaware that she and
Fabien had been together last night but she was soon
disillusioned.

'I believe that you and Fabien were caught on the
mountain in a storm,' said Rosine slyly. 'I hope you made
the most of it, Sophie. I'm quite sure that Fabien did.'

'You had better ask Fabien,' Sophie told her.

'I have,' Rosine admitted nonchalantly. 'He told me you
were *très gentille*. I wonder what he could have meant by
that?'

'I have no idea, Rosine,' Sophie said sharply.

Rosine's huge green eyes opened in exaggerated fashion.

'Don't sound so cross. Sophie. I don't mind if you spend
time with Fabien as long as he comes back to me. I know
him well and I know he would never fall in love with a cool
English miss. Besides you have your own boyfriend, *n'est-ce
pas?*'

'Yes, that is so,' Sophie told her.

She wished with all her heart that Rosine would go. She
was so possessive, so sure of Fabien. Last night Fabien had
just been getting his own back upon Rosine when he took
her, Sophie, up the mountain. It was just chance that he had
confided in her, and that tenderness and passion she
remembered were not really for her. Any other woman
would have been the same to him.

At last Rosine decided to depart.

'*Au 'voir*, Sophie *chérie*,' she said. 'I am shortly going to
London to do some shopping. I'll leave Fabien in your
hands. I'm sure you will take good care of him and that I
can trust you.'

And with a trill of silvery laughter, she was gone.

After this Sophie felt inclined to phone Fabien and
cancel their arrangement for tomorrow but she found she

could not do it. She wanted to see him again and to find out
how she felt when she met him in ordinary circumstances.
She told herself the surge of emotion she had felt when he
had told her his story was something like admiration
mingled with compassion. It could not on any account be
classed as love. But what was it that she had felt when he
had awakened her, when he had touched her hair, when she
had responded to his passionate kisses? No, that couldn't be
love, she told herself.

It was physical attraction brought on by all the
circumstances, the storm, their isolation on the mountains,
his peril when he had rescued the boy and the terrible story
he had told her. How fortunate that he had not responded
to her desire. He was Rosine's lover and, as she had said, she
knew how best to please him. What was it that Rosine had
said? That it was easy to manage a man if you had the right
technique. But she, Sophie, did not want to manage Fabien.
All she wanted was to love him.

This thought had come into her head without any
consideration of her previous reasoning, and she was
horrified. She tried to push it to the back of her mind. She
couldn't possibly love Fabien, who had consistently been
against her until yesterday. No, that thought was too
absurd. She must forget it immediately.

But when next morning, Fabien arrived to fetch her, she
felt a sudden leap of the heart as he came towards her
smiling and holding out his hands to take both of hers in his.

'Sophie, how enchanting you look this morning.'

She was wearing a blue dress that matched her eyes and
was sprigged all over with white daisies. Her copper hair
was loose on her shoulders, caught over her forehead by a
wide blue band. By now, through all her work in the
garden, her arms, legs and shoulders were a beautiful shade
of gold. Only where the dress showed part of her breasts
was there a small triangle of paler skin.

He seemed to have completely recovered from yesterday's ordeal and in his proud profile as he took the wheel
there seemed no trace of the humbled man who had

confessed to her the doubts of his own courage. It was just a mood, she thought. This arrogant-looking man is Fabien's true self and I had better remember that.

'Villefranche de Conflent first, I think,' he said.

'What is that?' Sophie asked.

'It's a very ancient town fortified from the eleventh century, built and rebuilt over and over again both in the thirteenth and seventeenth century, rugged buildings of pink marble and granite. Now it's a well-known tourist place but worth seeing nevertheless.'

They drove in the sunlight through beautiful vineyards, market gardens and orchards of blossoming pears, peaches, apricots and apples.

'Water has always been a problem here,' Fabien informed her. 'Winter rains are rare and the problem is to collect enough water from the mountain streams. Over the centuries there has been set up a magnificent network of irrigation channels. They say it dates back as far as when the Moors occupied the land. As you can see the whole landscape is dominated by the presence of Canigou, that mountain that towers over this country.'

'It seems very odd in all this sunlight to be able to see a mountain top in the distance that is still covered in snow.'

'We'll be nearer to Canigou when we arrive at the abbey of Saint Martin but first I must show you Villefranche.'

When they had parked the car and entered under the rounded stone archway of the ancient town, it was like going into a different world. From yesterday, Sophie had felt she was living in a kind of fairytale and this feeling increased as she saw this fabulous-looking place. The narrow streets, the old houses with red tiled roofs, all seemed to come from some old story. The shops were full of all kinds of exciting goods, things that she had not seen elsewhere, good things to eat, different kinds of paté, walnuts in all kinds of guise, walnut sweets, walnut chocolates, pickled walnuts, walnut oil, even walnut liqueur. They tasted some in a very small glass and it was so delicious that Fabien bought some for Sophie.

Coming back from their shopping into the main square at the entrance, Fabien suggested they should have a coffee or tisane and they sat under the plumy lilac blossoms of a wistaria that wound its way over a pergola. To add to the story-like quality of the day, a television crew had set up their cameras and taped music of a light opera was wafting towards them, while women and men in romantic costumes acted their parts against the background of the ancient town.

During a break in the proceedings, a very beautiful girl broke away from her fellow actors and came towards them. She was dressed in a crinoline of watered silk in shades of mulberry red and wore a very becoming poke bonnet over her silky blonde ringlets.

'Fabien, can it be you?'

Fabien rose smiling and kissed her on both cheeks.

'Corinne, how enchanting you look. You are still acting, then?'

She laughed delightfully.

'Yes, *méchant*, wicked one, I am still acting even though the years are passing too quickly.'

She turned to Sophie.

'And is this charming-looking creature your wife, Fabien? You have done well, *madame*, to capture such an elusive person as *le Comte*.'

'No, no, Corinne, I am still unmarried. This is Mademoiselle Sophie from England.'

'Oh, then you are still leaving your trail of broken hearts. Be warned, *mademoiselle*, Fabien is a hard man to pin down.'

Fabien laughed.

'You knew me in my wilder days, Corinne. I assure you I am a reformed character now.'

'I cannot believe that. This I can assure you, *mademoiselle*. He will leave you with some beautiful memories, but be warned, the operative word is "leave".'

She swam back to her fellow actors delicately lifting her crinoline in front of her.

'What a beautiful woman,' said Sophie.

'Ah, yes, possibly she is past her best now but at one time, when I knew her, she was considered one of the loveliest women in France.'

It was obvious, thought Sophie, that at one time they had had an intimate relationship. How many women had Fabien loved in his time? Even the most beautiful woman in France had fallen for his charms.

From Villefranche they headed towards the mountains and to St Martin de Canigou. They had to park the car at the bottom and start walking up the rough track that led to the monastery.

'This is what I meant by a penance,' Fabien said. 'I have forgotten how to walk. You are sure it will not tire you too much?'

But Sophie was very happy. The pleasant sunshine, not too hot today, the clear mountain air that was like sharp white wine, all contributed to her exhilaration. Beyond was the Massif de Canigou, the range of mountains with the impressive snow-covered Canigou towering over all the rest.

Half-way up they found a grassy place secluded from the road where they could eat their *déjeuner*. Far below they could see small villages and farms with solidly grouped buildings, the colour of the sun-warmed earth. Vines made neat patterns on the lower slopes and olive trees were dark green against the dry soil.

'It's beautiful,' breathed Sophie. 'How could you try to persuade me to live in a villa by the sea when there is all this here?'

'You may not have noticed, but I have stopped trying to persuade you, dear Sophie. I've decided I enjoy your company nearer at hand.'

She was touched by Fabien's declaration. Did he really not mind if she stayed at the *mas* now? But then she had another thought. How different it could be in the future if he married Rosine, as he seemed set to do. There would be no more excursions such as this one, no more intimate talks, no more passionate embraces. Passionate embraces that

lead nowhere, she told herself, or, if they did, they could
only lead to heartbreak. The beautiful Corinne was right to
warn me. But she shrugged off these thoughts and
determined to enjoy the day and not look any further.

She was here with Fabien and his brilliant smiles were
directed entirely at her, as he opened a bottle of bubbling
wine that had been cooled in a container of terracotta.
There were small bread rolls to be eaten with spiced ham
and roast chicken, and there was an exquisitely dressed
potato salad together with green salad and small red
radishes. A beautiful raspberry and red-currant tart
followed, all this accompanied by glasses of the sparkling
golden wine.

After lunch they fed the remains of the picnic to a couple
of white goats which had wandered up to them and then
they lay in the shade of the trees, looking over the hazy blue
of the mountains. Fabien began gently to stroke her arm
and Sophie felt shivers of delight penetrating deep down
into her body. She should not feel like this, she thought
hazily, but now he was kissing her and her mouth opened
submissively to his. She opened her eyes and saw his long
dark lashes over those dark brown inscrutable eyes and,
beyond his curling black hair, the blue mountains with
Canigou in the distance, austere and pure and reaching up
to the skies far away from all these betraying human
emotions.

'How lovely you are,' he said, as he cupped her breast in
his hands. 'As I told you, today is for penance, but tonight I
will make love to you in that beautiful bed that has been
known to so many passionate lovers. *Tu veux?*' he asked.
'You wish this?'

His hand was on her chin now turning her face to look
into his eyes and in them she could read a tender passionate
promise. She nodded unable to speak. She had commited
herself now, she thought, and yet she could still retreat. Did
she wish it? Did she wish he should make love to her when
all the time he was seemingly bound to Rosine? This
overwhelming attraction she felt for him was just, she

supposed, a well-known experience for him. He was used to women who felt this physical passion. It was not as it was for her, something utterly beyond her usual emotions.

As they continued their way up the mountain, he had his arm around her and she felt utterly happy with him. She wanted this day to last for ever, this lovely day far away from the ordinary world, up on the mountain where the breezes brought her the scent of lavender, of thyme and rosemary and marjoram, spicy and nostalgic. At last they reached the monastery sitting on the peak but with higher mountains behind reaching up to Canigou.

'After the Revolution, it was allowed to fall into ruin,' Fabien told her. 'But then it was rebuilt and the old stones and carvings used again.'

They followed the instructions to ring the bell three times. It became more and more like a fairy-tale, thought Sophie, as a monk came to welcome them with bright blue eyes that matched his gown.

'These are the Romanesque sculptures that you see here,' Fabien told her. 'This is the true art of Catalonia.'

The figures carved on the tops of the columns were very strange and beautiful, mythical beasts with wings, animal figures with bared fangs and curling locks, weird faces, yet alongside these some of the sculptures portrayed people living their ordinary life in the Middle Ages. To Sophie it was all enchanting, and she took careful photographs thinking that maybe she could write an article on Romanesque art to replace the profile of Fabien that she would never send. But then it was all new to her and she thought one would have to be an expert on the subject. So she decided to enjoy it without thinking how she could use it and walked around with Fabien who seemed delighted that she was so charmed with it.

Below them the landscape fell away into deep valleys and wild gorges and she thought what a contrast there was between the calm life of peace in the monastery and the rugged mountain scenery that was all around them. Inside the church against the rough stone of the walls there sat a

Virgin and Child painted in bright colours. Her red and gold robe contrasted with the blue of the Child's garment and each of them wore a gold crown. She looked peacefully out into her world as she had done for hundreds of years as if listening to the prayers of man.

Shadows were becoming longer and the mountains were smoky with the approach of evening as they made their way slowly down the steep path. Sophie felt lost in a dream. Every so often they would stop and embrace, and she felt that now she could never have enough of Fabien's kisses. She thought that she could be falling in love with him and yet she would not admit that to herself for she knew it could lead nowhere. As Corinne had said he would leave her with exquisite memories, but the operative word was 'leave'.

He was the most attractive man she had ever met and two days in his company had overwhelmed her common sense, she thought. He had vowed to make love to her tonight and at the thought of it she felt a shuddering sensation in her whole being. Feeling as she did now, it would be difficult to resist him, to deny her own emotions. Surrender would be so easy, denial too difficult. She felt envy for the blue-eyed monk who could live his life free from temptation high on his mountain top.

They drove home in the cool of the evening, every now and again holding each other's hand. Sophie's russet hair streamed out behind her in the slight breeze and the coolness seemed to bring her some peace from the thoughts that were tormenting her. They passed the granite walls of Villefranche, quiet now and free from the crowd of tourists, and she remembered Corinne again and her words of warning. They had left the forests behind and were driving through well-ordered vineyards with sometimes orchards in blossom. The litle farmhouses glowed in the golden light of the late afternoon as if their walls had taken life from the sun.

She began to think of the evening when they would arrive back at the *mas* and tried to occupy her mind with practical domestic things so as not to face the thought of the decision she must make. She dared not think of whether she could resist the temptation to respond to Fabien's passion with her own. Steadfastly she considered small things. She had left a casserole simmering in the oven at a very low heat. It would be ready to eat by the time they had arrived. She had asked Vidal to purchase a fresh baguette and some of those delicious little strawberry pies that one could buy at the *patisserie*. There would be wine too, perhaps not as good quality as Fabien was used to, but it would have to do. At least the coffee would be good.

She supposed that Fabien would be amused if he knew what thoughts were running through her head in place of the romantic dreams she had had during this long delicious day, but perhaps there would be more romantic dreams later. She would not think of that. As they drove over the rough road that led to the *mas*, she had never felt happier. These last two days had finally destroyed her hostility towards Fabien, and now she felt free to let his charm work, whatever the consequences. Forget Rosine, she thought, just for the present. She was happy with Fabien. That was all that mattered.

To Sophie the *mas* had never looked more beautiful as they arrived there. The sun, almost set now, still left its golden glow on the old walls and the cherry-trees were as beautiful as brides in their dresses of lacy white petals. As they walked over the patio, Fabien's hand on her arm, he said, 'Do you always leave the door open when you go out for the day?'

'Oh, no, that must be Vidal. He had done that before, forgotten to close it after he has been working inside. He has a room in the village now but he cannot have left it open for long. He usually works quite late.'

Sophie had no fears of intruders here now. She hardly thought it mattered that the door was open for she had complete trust in the villagers.

'It's what I would have expected from him,' grumbled Fabien. 'He's a careless wretch as I have told you before.'

'Don't let's quarrel over Vidal again,' Sophie implored, 'Especially today.'

Fabien's momentary anger disappeared and his hands were around her shoulders as they made their way into the living-room of the *mas*. The sun had set and the whole room appeared to be in shadow, the only light now from the small windows and a flicker of flame from the wood stove that she had asked Vidal to tend during the day. A figure rose from the old chair near to the table where papers and notebooks were set.

'Sophie. You're here at last.'

Sophie could hardly see his face, but she recognised that voice. She ran towards him and he swept her up into a bear-like embrace, then, laughing at her surprise, set her down.

'Mike, what on earth are you doing here? Why didn't you tell me you were coming?'

'I hadn't time. I'm on a business trip to Perpignan but I thought since I was going to be so near I'd have a chance to visit you. Just a flying call. I've ordered a car to take me back to Perpignan at five a.m. tomorrow. I knew you wouldn't refuse me a bed for the night.'

'Of course not,' cried Sophie.

Oh, why did he come today? she thought. Any other time she would have been delighted to end to see him, but not on this day that had promised to end on a perfect note. She turned to Fabien. He was still standing by the door and his expression had completely changed. He was again the man she had met in the beginning, the aloof aristocrat who wanted nothing to do with the outside world.

'Oh, Fabien,' she said now. 'I was so surprised that I have forgotten my manners. This is Mike Kingsford, he is my ...' Her voice trailed away. How could she admit at this late stage that she was one of the tribe of hated journalists and that Mike was her editor? 'He is a good friend of mine,' she added lamely.

'So it would appear,' sneered Fabien, his voice icy.

'And this is Fabien de Cressac, Mike.'

She was terribly aware of Fabien's anger. Surely he

could not suspect her, and yet it appeared he did.

'The Comte de Cressac,' said Mike easily. 'Ah, yes, I have heard of you.'

'But I have never heard of you, *monsieur*. It seems I was not supposed to know of your existence.'

'Oh, I wouldn't say that. I shouldn't expect Sophie would discuss our relationship when she is away on vacation. Sophie is a free spirit and lives at a rate when she is in London. I'm happy for her to get away for a while and find relaxation elsewhere.'

'Very modern way of thinking. She appears to have done that very successfully,' Fabien told him. 'And now I must leave you to discuss whatever dear friends do who have been parted for all of two weeks. Goodbye, Sophie. What is your English saying? Two is company, three's a crowd.'

He strode to the door and, before she could speak to him, he had leapt into his car and started to drive away, although she called after him, but he either did not hear or did not want to hear.

'So that's the famous Comte de Cressac,' Mike said when she returned. 'He sure lived up to his reputation now, didn't he? Not exactly overflowing with human kindness, but you seem to have managed to make some impression on him, Sophie.'

'Not a lot, Mike,' Sophie told him sadly. 'As you see he is very handsome and he can be charming.'

She felt devastated by this turn of events but she could not tell Mike this. If she told him she thought she was falling in love with Fabien, her hard-headed editor would think her crazy. How could she hope to explain to Fabien that Mike was her employer without disclosing that she herself was a journalist? Fabien had been furiously angry. He obviously thought that Mike was her lover and Mike had not made it any easier by the way he had spoken about her, for Fabien could not realise he was referring to her working life.

Then another thought occurred to her and she felt as if an icy hand had touched her spine. She had told Rosine that her boy-friend was named Mike Kingsford. It was the first name that had entered her head. She could imagine that Fabien would go straight from here to see Rosine. It was the kind of revenge he would take if he were angry with her, Sophie. And Rosine would be very pleased to tell him that Mike was the name of her lover. What a fool she had been! She had set a trap for herself.

'How are you getting on with your profile of *M. le Comte*?' asked Mike. 'You seem to be getting plenty of opportunities to study him.'

'Oh, I've done some notes but I haven't got it together yet,' Sophie told him.

She would approach him later about not wanting to write the article. At the moment she felt so depressed by Fabien's attitude that she could not have a showdown with Mike. She knew he would be annoyed with her that she would not do it and he would try to persuade her otherwise, and she could not face an argument right now.

'Something in that oven smells delicious, Sophie,' he said now. 'How about my opening this bottle of wine I've brought. You can have that but I guess I need a Scotch. I've had a hectic day interviewing various people. I hired a car to get here and it took a devil of a lot of finding, but the same man is calling for me at crack of dawn. I have one or two things to finish in Perpignan and then I must catch my plane so I guess I'll have an early night. You look all in too. Has that Count been giving you the runaround?'

'Not exactly,' Sophie told him. 'He's quite a difficult character, as you said.'

'Well, don't let it get you down, but I would like to have that profile to go in with the new season's attempt on the north wall of the Eiger. It will be starting as soon as the weather clears there, I expect.'

Sophie didn't reply. She would tell him about her decision later. At least, she thought, there was someone to appreciate her casserole for she herself had small appetite. Mike ate heartily talking all the time so that she didn't need to exert herself to entertain him. He did not refer to Fabien

again or to the article so she thought he had been satisfied
with her explanation. She would tell him just before he left
in the morning that she did not intend to go on with her
plans. That way she could hope to avoid too much of a
confrontation. They sat talking for a while and then she
thought he looked exhausted.

'Would you like my bed?' she asked. 'And I'll sleep on the
settee.'

'Certainly not. I wouldn't dream of it. I assure you that,
after my years as a foreign correspondent, I can sleep
anywhere.'

He offered to come and help her carry the bedding in
from her room and, when he saw the romantic bed, he said,
'Wow, Sophie, it's a great pity you're here alone. That bed
calls for a couple of lovers. It looks as if it could have plenty
of tales to tell.'

'Without a doubt,' said Sophie. 'It belonged to the old
Count. He used to entertain his mistresses here.'

'And the present Count? Does he lead an equally
exciting life?'

'It's possible,' said Sophie repressively. 'He wants to buy
the *mas* from me. For what purpose I don't know.'

'Indeed? And are you considering it?'

'Certainly not. I'll go on with the renovations however
much he tries to stop me.'

Again she was feeling bitter towards Fabien. Who would
have thought she could feel like this again after the two
glorious days they had spent together? But she was
depressed by his obvious anger at Mike's arrival, and let's
face it, she thought, she was disappointed at the unexpected
end to the day. Why hadn't he waited to be given some
explanation of Mike's presence? But then what could she
have said? She would have been in even deeper waters if
she had revealed that Mike was the editor of a well-known
journal and that she worked for him.

She made up the bed for Mike and very soon he was in a
deep sleep, but she herself could not settle. It was not truly
dark tonight and she wandered outside in the bright

starlight under the white ermine of the cherry-trees. The petals fell like snow on to her hair and settled in patches of white on the dewy grass. In the hedge a nightingale was singing its heart out. She lay in the hammock that she had found in the cellar and had got Vidal to string between two trees, and she looked at the stars, brilliant spots of light against the dark azure of the night sky.

She found that, in spite of her bitterness towards Fabien, she now longed for his presence. If only things could have continued as they were. In the middle of the starlit night, she needed him to be there with her, but the spell had been broken. She was back in the ordinary difficult world again and she didn't know how she could ever hope to get back to that fairy-tale world she had inhabited with Fabien for just a day. She could not stand the direction of her thoughts, and assured herself that it was impossible she could love him. She could not fall in love with a man who was so completely domineering and unreasonable.

At last she made her way back to the house and in desperation took a sleeping-pill. Mike had assured her that she need not get up when the car arrived for him, but she would be sure to wake. When she had obtained these pills one time when she had been ill, the doctor had assured her they had very little effect, but, as it happened, she had never needed to take one before. It was true they did not seem very effective, she thought, as she tossed and turned for another hour, hearing a curlew calling its melancholy note echoing her own sad heart, but eventually she slept.

CHAPTER NINE

SOPHIE awoke reluctantly. She felt as if she had been on a journey of many miles. Something must have awakened her for she still felt as if she could close her eyes again and sleep for hours. Yes, it was the sound of Vidal hammering on the roof outside. Vidal? But he only came at eight in the morning. He couldn't be here now. She still had to see that Mike got away to the airport on time. But it was Vidal and when she looked at her watch, she could not believe that it was half-past eight already. She staggered out of the bed and surveyed the other room. Everything was neat and tidy, the blankets folded and placed on the settee together with the pillow. Coffee was set on the side of the stove and one of the large pottery bowls had been washed and left on the sink.

A note was propped against the jug of milk on the table and she opened it, feeling ashamed that she had overslept and not been there to say goodbye to Mike.

'You were sleeping so peacefully that I didn't want to disturb you,' she read. 'In any case there was no need. I know how to manage for myself from years of practice, but I have a confession to make. When I was looking for paper to write this, I found your notes on the subject of de Cressac and I have taken them for I feel they are good enough for me to whip into shape without demanding any more work from you on the subject. Last night I thought you looked tired and, as you told me before, this is supposed to be your vacation.'

'In fact I thought your notes were outstandingly good as they stood even though you said they were unfinished, and, as the new Eiger North Face attempts will be news shortly and the post here cannot be too reliable, it's best that I should take the article as it stands. Don't worry, Sophie, as

usual you have done a very good job. There are only one or
two ends to tie up. I'll send you the cheque as soon as a
publication date is set. You won't get any less because the
article was unfinished, I can assure you.'

Sophie felt as if she had been plunged into a bath of cold
water. Outside the hot sun was turning the air to a
shimmering rainbow, but here, even though the stove had
been lit, she felt a deathly chill. She had never intended that
Mike should have that article. She had just written about
Fabien for her own benefit, an intimate memoir of all he
had said to her, an admiring memoir certainly but not for
publication. She tried to collect her muddled thoughts. She
should never have let Mike think she was getting on with
the profile. She should have told him last night that she
didn't want to do it. And now what was to happen? But
there must be something she could do. Mike had said he had
some things to do in Perpignan before catching the plane. If
she went to the airport she might still be in time to catch
and implore him not to use it.

She flung on her clothes, not waiting even to drink
coffee, and told Vidal she had to go to Perpignan on urgent
business. She heard him shouting after her, urging her to
buy some of the materials he needed, but she took no notice.
That would have to wait for another time, and besides, her
funds were low. She drove along the main highway,
pressing her little car to the limit. She must stop Mike, she
thought, even if it meant losing her job, for he was quite
capable of dismissing her if she opposed the publication of
this article. Once he had had an idea for one and he could
see it would connect with present news, she knew it would
be hard to make him see that she didn't want it published.

The traffic was heavy and she had to slow down once she
got upon the road leading to the airport. At last, after
having to park the car, she rushed into the departure
lounge. Unlike the usual busy scene that greeted one at
airports, this one seemed totally quiet. She seemed quite
alone in the place, but she could see one plane on the
runway. She felt so desperate that she tried to make her way

out there on to the tarmac, but found that the doors leading out were locked. At last she found an official.

'The plane for Gatwick, what time does it depart?' she demanded.

The sleepy-looking man took his time at answering her in heavy accented French hard to understand.

'There's only one today, mademoiselle, and that is just leaving. The doors are closed and it is taking off. It's too late to catch it now.'

As he was speaking, she saw the plane taxi along the runway and raise itself into the air. Soon it was a tiny silver speck high in the sky.

She sat down on a bench and put her head in her hands. What was she to do now? She had missed Mike by a few minutes, and she felt completely frustrated. But she would have to get in touch with him somehow before he put this thing in operation. She knew the speed with which he was accustomed to work when he had had what he thought was a brilliant idea and she would have to be quick to stop him. Her only hope would be to ring him when he arrived back. It would be difficult to persuade him not to publish when she was speaking on the phone, but he would have to take notice of her. Either way she would have to face an angry man and she would rather endure Mike's anger even if it meant dismissal than face Fabien's hurt and anger at her breach of confidence.

Mike would not be home for hours yet and she felt too distraught to go back and have to wait until she could get in touch with him. She would drive into Perpignan, park the car somewhere and have a look round. Not that she really wanted to, but maybe it would distract her mind from her troubles. She knew a little about the city because Fabien had told her that it had been the capital of a separate state, the home of the kings of Majorca, and it had not been incorporated into France until 1659. In the Roussillon, he had told her, all roads lead to Perpignan, whether they come from the plain, the sea or the mountains.

She thought of this as she drove in past the market

gardens with their apricot and peach-trees, their blossoms
glowing in the sun, then into a place of little white houses,
with the bell tower of a church showing pale crimson
behind them. Beyond the town in the distance Canigou still
dominated the landscape with its far-off snows. Sophie did
not want to look at this for it would only remind her of how
happy she had been yesterday.

She found a place to park her car and wandered rather
distractedly about the narrow busy streets. It was no use
trying to get away from her thoughts for they continued to
pursue her. One disaster seemed to have been closely
followed by another; first, Fabien had got completely the
wrong idea about Mike's arrival at the *mas*, and now, far
worse, there was the threat that Mike might publish the
intimate profile she had written about Fabien. She might
eventually be able to explain Mike's presence to Fabien,
but he would certainly never forgive her if that article
appeared in print. She braced herself to try to think how
she could persuade Mike on the phone that it was not on to
publish it. But would he take any notice of her wishes? She
knew what he was like when he was after a scoop. He would
let nothing stand in his way.

She had now come to a kind of square where she noticed
people were sitting at tables and being served with
refreshments, and she remembered that she had not had
anything to eat or drink since last night and hardly
anything then. No wonder she felt dizzy. She found a
vacant table on the edge of the crowd and, sitting down,
ordered black coffee, then looked around her. The ancient
building nearby had on its roof a model of a ship in full sail
and queer gargoyles looking down from on high.

'What is that place?' she asked the waiter when he
brought the pot of coffee.

'The Loge de Mer, *mademoiselle*. It was the old maritime
offices as you can see. It is very old. Perpignan has very
many old and elegant buildings.'

She drank her coffee slowly, feeling she must linger until
it was time to get on the phone and plead with Mike. What

had possessed her to write those notes? But it was her usual way when anything had impressed her to write it down. She had never dreamed that Mike would arrive on her doorstep and walk off with them. She looked at the people sitting at adjacent tables. They all looked so happy without a care in the world. And she herself had been happy, oh, so happy, until Mike had arrived. Remembering Fabien's thunderous expression when he had met Mike, Sophie thought that no amount of explanation would ever let him get over his anger with her. It was too ridiculous that she should be suspected of having a love affair with Mike of all people, but, if he didn't know the truth about their relationship, of course Fabien would think the worst, and there was nothing she could explain without getting into further trouble.

She could see a dark-haired man of strong build moving through the crowd and she thought how strange it was that, when you were very emotionally involved with someone, you often imagined that you could see them when all the time it was someone else, someone probably completely different when they drew nearer. The man glanced up and stopped as if something strange had shocked him, then came straight towards her. It was Fabien, and at once Sophie's heart described a jittery leap and then started beating far too fast. He stood over her, his expression enigmatic.

'Alone, Sophie? May I sit down.'

'Please do,' she said.

She looked at his arrogant profile turned away from her as he ordered fresh coffee from the waiter, the long lashes above the brilliant eyes, the arched brows and the dark tendrils of hair tangled with the gold medallion above the open neck of the white shirt, so familiar to her, so dear. I'm crazy but I love him, she admitted to herself. I can't let this happen to him, this publicity that Mike is determined to give him again. He suffered enough in the past for this story. It can't be raked up again for another news sensation.

'So, your *cher ami* has departed, Sophie. Too bad it was such a flying visit.'

'He is not what you mean by a *cher ami*, Fabien,' she denied. 'He is a friend. Only that.'

'I wish I could believe you, Sophie, with your so-innocent deep blue eyes, but he did not give me that impression. I felt you had some very intimate relationship. I don't think you can deny that.'

'Yes, but . . .' said Sophie.

This was all too difficult. Of course their relationship would appear intimate to a stranger, someone who did not know it was bound up with the work they did together.

'And what brought you into Perpignan? I thought your friend said he had arranged a car for the morning.'

'Yes, he did,' said Sophie. 'But I remembered something I wanted to say to him and I went to the airport to try to catch him. Unfortunately I was too late.'

Fabien regarded her with a mocking smile.

'And you say you do not have a romantic interest in him, yet you are willing to pursue him for all these miles just to give him some last message? What was this message then? It must have been most important.'

'I can't tell you. It was something just between me and him.'

She could tell she had only made matters worse with Fabien. She could not tell him the truth and any other explanation sounded as if Mike was her lover and she hadn't been able to bear to part from him.

'Don't try to bluff me, Sophie. Rosine said to me that you yourself told her her you were in love with someone called Mike Kingsford, and it was self-evident the way you greeted each other that that was true.'

'But why should that make you so angry?' Sophie demanded. 'It has nothing to do with you because it is very evident that you are in love with Rosine. She too is your *petite amie*. That much is clear to me.'

Fabien's face was dark with an angry scowl.

'Whom I am in love with is entirely my own affair. What has made me so angry is the way you deceived me. I thought you were lovely and innocent. You let me hope to

make love to you without saying one word about this Mike.
That is what I can't forgive.'

'And you hoped to make love to me without reminding
me that you were committed to Rosine, so that makes us a
pair,' said Sophie angrily.

Suddenly to her astonishment the whole world started
spinning around her.

'Why is it getting so dark?' she asked Fabien and
collapsed in a dead faint.

She came to to find herself reclining on a couch in the
foyer of a restaurant to which presumably she had been
carried. The large patronne dressed in tight black satin was
waving a bottle of some kind of smelling-salts under her
nose and making her sneeze, and she could see Fabien
behind her holding a glass of brandy.

'I don't think I must have any of that,' she told him
weakly. 'I'm not in the habit of doing this, but I've had
practically nothing to eat since the lunch we had yesterday
and I've been wandering around Perpignan for ages before
I sat down to that coffee.'

'Good grief, you really must be in love,' said Fabien, but
the anger seemed to have gone from his expression and
instead he was looking concerned, as any man would, she
thought, if a woman stopped the argument by fainting in
front of him.

He spoke to the *patronne* and she came hurrying with
some delicious-tasting chicken broth with savoury croutons
floating in it. She fed it to Sophie as if she were a child while
Fabien looked on. She felt completely revived by it and,
when the *patronne* suggested she should eat something else,
she sat at a table with Fabien and, while he ate a steak with
pommes frites, she nibbled at some pieces of fish that were
delicately cooked. She refused the wine he offered but had
some more reviving coffee. Soon she felt able to smile at him
and he seemed to have forgotten his anger.

'I'm sorry about that,' she told him. 'I've never done such
a thing before but now I feel completely recovered.'

'Well now, I don't think you should drive yet. Would you

like to come with me to see the palace of the kings of
Majorca? It won't be too fatiguing, I promise you. It's one
of the sights of Perpignan.'

It was quite ridiculous but she began to feel happy again
just because he had stopped being angry with her and he
was suggesting that she should spend some time with him.
But she must get back in time to phone Mike. Yet she
hesitated to say so because she didn't want to bring up the
subject of Mike again when he seemed to have forgotten
about it. Mike couldn't possibly be at the office yet. She
would phone him this evening at his home.

As they walked through the old city, Sophie noticed
elegant houses that must date from a long time ago.

'This is a royal city,' Fabien told her. 'It used to be the
home of kings.'

She thought he too could have been a king, as he strode
beside her, not seeming to notice the admiring glances of
the people he passed. At last they came to the palace with its
enormous fortifications with towers at four corners leading
into an inner courtyard. There were few people about at
this time and Sophie was very conscious in this vast
building that she was alone with Fabien, as alone as she had
been on the mountain. There were great archways of stone
high up in the roof with dark beams holding the red
interior tiles in the throne-room and the air struck chill
from the red shining tiles of the floor beneath. She shivered
and felt Fabien's arm warm around her shoulders.

'I shouldn't have made you walk. You are still unwell.'

'No, no, I am quite recovered,' Sophie told him.

But she shouldn't be here with Fabien, she thought, she
should be driving home to try to get a message to Mike. But
it was too early yet, she told herself. This evening would be
soon enough. She could not forgo this time with Fabien
when she had thought before that he wanted nothing more
to do with her.

They wandered into the beautiful chapel. This too had a
roof that was tiled inside and she commented on it.

'That's very typical of the way of building in the

Roussillon. Even your own ceiling should be lined with tiles if it is to be typical of a Catalan *mas*. They have probably dropped off with age, but they could be replaced. It would be fairly costly but it would be worth it for true authenticity.'

Sophie sighed. It brought her back to the fact that her money was running out and that all the materials were proving too expensive, let alone thinking of lining the roof with expensive red tiles.

'I should be going back,' she said reluctantly.

He took her back to the place where she had parked her car, but, before she could turn on the ignition, he leaned over her and taking her chin in his hand he looked deeply into her eyes. His gaze seemed to hold her transfixed so that she could not look away.

'Sophie, tell me, do you truly love this man?'

She did not ask what man for she knew he was referring to Mike.

She shook her head and his hand dropped away then came up to smooth her face. At his touch something trembled deep in her being as if a bird had fluttered there.

'There is no love between us, Fabien, only liking.'

His eyes still held hers and he seemed to be considering something.

'Are you going to ask me for supper tonight? Remember I missed my promised meal last night. I presume your friend ate it instead. We can pick up some food at a *charcuterie* and a bottle of wine and I can follow you home to see that you get there safely after your earlier mishap.'

It was what she wanted to do most of all in the world and yet she could not do it. If he followed her now and came home with her, then when was she going to have the opportunity to phone Mike? She could not do it in his hearing. Perhaps she could ask him to come later, but then maybe she would not be able to get Mike at first.

'I'm sorry, Fabien, I can't have you to supper tonight,' she told him.

His hand dropped to his side and his eyes, that had been

brilliant and laughing, became hard as stone.

'You have another engagement?' he asked.

'No, but I have to make a phone call. It's very important.'

'And obviously very private. Is it to Mike?'

Sophie felt herself blushing. She could feel the blood rushing to her cheeks betraying her.

Fabien's lips, those lips that she had known so well upon her own, were straight and rigid in a severe line.

'You need not tell me, Sophie. Your expression had admitted it already. He has only just left and you cannot wait to be in touch with him again, and yet you say he is not your lover. What do you expect me to believe now?'

'I don't expect you to believe anything,' cried Sophie. 'You obviously want to expect the worst of me, and there doesn't seem anything I can do about it, so I'll go.'

And with that she put her car into gear and drove away leaving Fabien on the pavement. She caught a glimpse of him in the rear mirror and he was waving to her to stop and looking furious but she drove on. She should never have consented to spend the afternoon with him. It had only made things worse. He had seemed more kindly disposed to her but that was only probably because she had fainted and appealed to his more courteous instincts. He seemed obsessed with the idea that she was in love with Mike, but she could not explain the position without betraying her profession and it should hardly matter to him for he was in love with Rosine, but she expected his vanity was touched because she had appeared to be attracted to him.

What a muddle it all was, and Mike had made it worse by taking those notes of hers. She did not look forward to speaking to him. It would be difficult to make him see her point of view.

But, when she tried Mike's number, she drew a blank. After struggling to get through for a long time, she finally contacted an operator.

'Oh, haven't you heard, *mademoiselle*? There have been heavy storms in the mountains and some lines are down. They maybe won't be fully restored until tomorrow or later. At the moment you can only send and receive local calls.'

'When did this happen?' Sophie asked.

'Just a little while ago, *mademoiselle*.'

So, if she had come straight home instead of going around Perpignan with Fabien, she might have got through to Mike.

Now she had offended Fabien for nothing, and this time he would find it hard to forgive her. But worse, if she could not get in touch with Mike and he went ahead with publishing that article, she would be in deep trouble with Fabien and it would be all her own fault.

She kept trying Mike's number in spite of what the operator had said, late into the night but at last she gave up and, flinging herself down utterly exhausted, she fell into a deep sleep.

CHAPTER TEN

As it happened, it was two days before the lines were restored and Sophie had spent an anxious time trying to get through to London but never succeeding. When she finally heard Mike's voice, she felt so confused she hardly knew what to say, but she pulled herself together and quickly explained to Mike that she did not want the article to be pulished.

'I can't be hearing you right,' Mike protested. 'It's by far the best thing you've done even if it wasn't polished as much as you intended. You can be sure I saw to that. I'm sure you would be pleased with the way I edited it.'

'But don't you understand, Mike? I just did those notes for my own benefit. But it was no good. I never intended the profile should be published.'

'I can't understand you, Sophie. It's not like you to be so modest. It was well worth publishing and it looks very well in today's issue. I even found some old photographs of the *Comte*.'

'What?'

'Oh, yes, Sophie. There was a big item of news about a new assualt on the North Face so I worked on it as soon as I arrived back yesterday and it appeared this morning.'

'Then it's too late to stop it,' Sophie said dully.

She was clutching the phone as if it were a lifeline but now it could not save her.

'Far too late,' Mike agreed. 'As a matter of fact, I've had some congratulations on it already. It has created quite a sensation. Before this de Cressac faded completely out of the news, but now he's back right in the forefront. You'll probably have reporters descending on you in that *mas* of yours. Your peace and quiet will be ruined and a good thing too. It might make you hurry back here all the sooner.'

'Perhaps I shall,' Sophie told him.

She felt she wanted to turn tail and run now. What was going to happen when Fabien learned of her deception, as she was sure he would? But need this be so? The article had only been published in London and surely it would be unlikely that any reporter would come here now? Mike was exaggerating as usual. She had told Fabien's story in full. There was nothing more to be said about it. The echoes of the article might not reach into this quiet valley. But, even if Fabien never found out, she would always feel guilty that it was because of her that his intimate secrets had been told.

The phone rang and she started guiltily, but it was not Fabien but Germaine.

'My dear Sophie, we have not seen you for a while. Belle is unwell and would like it very much if you would visit us. We will have afternoon tea this afternoon in the English fashion. Do come and join us. It would give my poor Belle so much pleasure.'

Sophie was embarrassed. If Fabien was still angry with her, she wondered whether she should risk meeting him once more, but she could not refuse Germaine's polite request and she wanted to see Fabien. In spite of everything, she longed to see him once more, for, if he found out what she had done, she knew that would be the end to their friendship.

'Thank you, Germaine, I should like that,' she answered.

Once more she drove along the tree-lined avenue to the château. Today the skies were overcast and the towering stone walls had an air of greyness and gloom unlike the first day she had seen it, when the sunlit walls had reflected the radiance of sunshine. The peacocks stalked across the wide lawns uttering their harsh cries like souls in torment crying out for help, but once inside the salon all was light and warmth. A log fire reflected on the silver fire-irons and the gold-silk curtains seemed to replace the lack of sunlight. Great bowls of lilacs on the numerous small tables filled the air with their fragrance.

Belle was lying upon a daybed that was pulled up to the fire. She was dressed in her usual black with white frills at wrist and throat but she had a lacy wool shawl about her shoulders and a fluffy rug upon her knees. She looked very frail and very old but she smiled and her silver curls bobbed under the white lace cap as she greeted Sophie.

'Sophie, how good to see you. That naughty Fabien seems to want to keep you all to himself, but today he is hard at work, so we will have an opportunity for talk ourselves, *n'est-ce pas?*'

That is a relief, thought Sophie, and yet she felt a sharp pang of disappointment that she was not to see Fabien.

Bernadette came in with a laden trolley and made tea over a spirit stove with a silver teapot. There were thin cucumber sandwiches, tiny scones and exquisite small cakes and petit fours, all, thought Sophie, as it would have been in England in Edwardian times. She thought of the way, when she was at work, she grabbed a mug of tea and drank it while concentrating on the subject in hand. This seemed another world.

'We are so glad that you have been seeing something of Fabien,' Germaine told her. 'He needs company to help him be a little less serious. He is not, you understand, as he used to be when he was younger. He was perhaps a little wild but then many young men are so. It makes us sad that he has not yet married. He needs someone gentle and intelligent, someone who would understand him, someone *comme il faut.*'

'Someone like you, my dear Sophie,' Belle put in eagerly.

'Don't embarrass the girl, Belle,' said Germaine sharply.

'I do not intend to embarrass her, Germaine. It is lovely, *n'est-ce pas*, for a girl to be able to blush these days. You understand, Sophie, Fabien was wild in his youth, but not any more. My dear Aristide was wild also. That was why dear Papa disapproved.'

'Yes, yes, Belle, we know about Aristide. You have told us too often,' cried Germaine impatiently. 'Now we are talking about Sophie and Fabien. We want you to know, dear Sophie, that we like you very much and that if you and Fabien . . . well, you would have our full approval.'

Sophie felt deeply touched, but at the same time horribly embarrassed.

'I don't think Fabien thinks of me in that way at all,' she stammered. 'And what of Rosine?'

'Rosine?' Germaine's eyes narrowed. 'No, I do not think so. A *petite amie*, maybe, but not a wife.'

And they would not approve of her as a prospective bride for Fabien, thought Sophie, if they knew that she had disclosed his life story to the press. Poor old dears. They probably were terribly eager to marry Fabien off so that he would produce children before they died and they had fastened on to her because they did not approve of Rosine. She was probably too modern for them, and they perhaps feared she would want them to live elsewhere if she were to marry Fabien.

'Sophie,' said Belle shyly, 'I have a request to make to you, a particular favour.'

'You are at liberty to refuse. Belle shouldn't really worry you with her romantic nonsense,' Germaine declared.

'What is it, Belle?' Sophie asked. 'I'm most willing to do anything if it's in my power.'

She felt sorry for this very fragile-looking old lady who looked as if a puff of breeze could blow her away.

'I'd like to see you in the dress I wore when Aristide painted my portrait. My colouring was not unlike yours when I was young, dark blue eyes and hair the colour of the beech-trees in autumn. That is how Aristide described it. But now my eyes are faded and my hair is quite white, yet I have a wish, a longing to see this dress I so loved on someone young and beautiful. It will remind me of so many good things, the loveliest time of my life.'

Her weak voice died away on a sigh.

'Of course I'll wear it if it will give you pleasure,' Sophie assured her.

'It's a very nonsensical notion she has,' Germaine

whispered, 'but she is far from well and I think we should take notice of her wishes. Bernadette has set out the dress in the small salon next door and you will find the accessories there too, the shoes, the gloves, the fan. There is a mirror where you will be able to see yourself. It would be doing her a kindness if you would dress yourself in these clothes for a while.'

Germaine sent Bernadette to help her and, as Sophie stripped off her own few garments, the old *bonne* handed her the white silk stockings, the cream satin shoes, the voluminous petticoat, the laced bodice. The dress was beautiful still, a creation of creamy silk and lace draped low at the neck displaying Sophie's golden neck and shoulders and the paler cream of her breasts. She could not believe it was really she when she looked at last into the long gilt mirror. The reflection that looked back at her seemed like something from an old romance, perhaps Cinderella before she went to the ball, certainly nothing to do with Sophie, modern girl and successful journalist.

'I knew she would look as I did,' said Belle, clapping her hands in delight. 'What do you say, Germaine, isn't she charming? Aristide would have wanted to paint her just like this.'

'Certainly you look very beautiful, Sophie,' Germaine said. 'Thank you for doing this for Belle. As you can see she is very pleased. As for me, the past is a forgotten country, but for Belle it is real and her life now is fading. She lives in those far-off days, so it was kind of you to do this for her.'

'Ah, here is Fabien,' Belle cried. 'He has finished his work earlier than he expected. What do you think, Fabien? Is Sophie not lovelier than ever?'

He had stopped in the doorway and his eyes seemed to Sophie darker and more intense than she had ever seen them. Then he smiled, that charming smile that she had grown to love. Had he forgotten his displeasure with her now? But if he only knew, he had a far deeper cause for anger.

'Yes, indeed, Belle, she looks truly beautiful, as beautiful as you must have looked when Aristide painted you.'

'Of course. I would have liked to see her beside those paintings,' her voice faltered. 'But I have forgotten where they are.'

'Let's hope they will be found some day,' Fabien told her.

'Are they lost then? I thought ...'

There was such distress in her voice that Germaine quickly intervened.

'Dear Belle, you said that, when Sophie dressed, you would like to see her in the château ballroom where you first wore the dress.'

Belle clapped her hands. She had forgotten the mystery of the paintings.

'Oh, yes, and now that Fabien is here, I would like to see them dance as I danced with Aristide. It was not my first ball for then, you remember, Germaine, I wore white, but it was the most thrilling ball we ever had, when Aristide took me into the garden and declared his love. The lilac was in bloom then just as it is now. Its fragrance brings it all back to me. Dear Sophie, will you do this for me?'

Sophie looked at Fabien and saw him nod slightly.

'Of course,' she agreed. 'But what do we do for music?'

'There is an old record-player there and some Strauss waltzes,' Fabien told her. 'I should think that would satisfy Belle.'

The ballroom was across the hall from the salon, shuttered and dark, the gilt chairs piled in twos and threes around the walls, but, when the crystal chandeliers were lit, they gave off a soft, ghostly glimmer that illuminated the middle of the room leaving the rest shadowed, the gold-framed mirrors, the stage with its rose-velvet curtains, the gilded cupids holding lamps in each corner of the room. There seemed to Sophie to be a fragrance of long-dead flowers mingled with dust.

As Fabien started the old player, the sweet sound of a waltz echoed around the room and he took Sophie into his arms. Again she was startled by the effect his touch had on her. She fought to remain calm but it was no good. His hand was on the thin silk at her waist seeming to burn through to her skin. She looked up at him and saw that his eyes were upon her compelling her to respond to his touch, and now they seemed to turn in the rhythm of the dance as if they were one person.

She heard the sound of thin clapping from the corner of the room and still she felt she never wanted the dance to end, but the music stopped and Germaine came towards them.

'Thank you, Sophie, that was beautiful, and now I think I should take Belle for a rest. She has had quite enough excitement for one day.'

'Thank you Sophie,' Belle echoed in a thin, tired voice. 'And please, for my sake, have one more waltz before you finish. You dance so beautifully together as I knew you would.'

Sophie looked up at Fabien and he was smiling.

'Very well, Aunt Belle, we shall,' Fabien assured her.

They were dancing again but now Sophie was very conscious that they were alone in the elegant, dimly lit ballroom. The ghosts of all the others who had danced here seemed to press around her, other people who had been happy here, all those who had found love as they waltzed to the romantic tunes of Strauss.

'You are so lovely, Sophie. I will make you forget this Mike. I will make you belong to me, only me, do you hear?'

He had stopped dancing and his arms were fiercely embracing her, his kisses burning on her bare golden shoulders and the low bosom of her dress, then strong and deep on her mouth. In all her being she felt the strength of his desire and all she wanted was to respond to him, to be carried on to some high wave of bliss that she felt could be theirs.

And then the spell was broken. There was a discreet cough from the doorway of the room and Fabien let her go, but still one arm was around her and she clung to his hand as if she did not ever want to let him go.

'What is it, Gaston?' Fabien demanded angrily from the

manservant. 'Can't it wait?'

The servant was standing with discreetly downcast eyes.

'A phone call from London, *M. le Comte*, Mademoiselle Rosine wishes to speak to you.'

'Tell her ...' Fabien began impatiently. 'No, no, I suppose I'd better take it myself.'

At the mention of London, Sophie's heart had taken a plunge. She had forgotten that Rosine was in London. But was it likely she would read an English journal? No, she had probably just phoned Fabien in the usual course of things. But she, Sophie, must come out of her dream. This couldn't be her, this woman in the romantic ball-dress who had responded so eagerly to Fabien's murmurs of desire. She was the woman who had written the article that would rouse Fabien's anger if he were ever to find out. She was a journalist and one of the tribe that Fabien had learned to hate. There was no future for her with Fabien, however much she was attracted to him.

Fabien had not come back. Slowly she went back to the small salon and changed back into her own clothes. The dream was over before it had even properly begun. She must go back to the *mas* now, back to the task of trying to find how she was to finance the repairs. She remembered with a shocked feeling that she would be paid for the article she had never intended to be published, but felt she could not take it. It would be like receiving thirty pieces of silver. How could she ever bring herself to use it?

She thought she would manage to slip quietly away from the château. Fabien must be taking the phone call in his own apartment, but then, as she began to cross the hall to the heavy oak door, she heard his voice upon the stairs.

'Sophie, just a moment, please.'

She stayed where she was, feeling as if she had been encased in ice. The tone of his voice could mean only one thing. Slowly she turned and met the black frown of his eyes as he came towards her. He put his hands on her shoulders grasping them in a fierce grip so that she was forced to keep on looking at him and could not turn away from that terrible gaze.

'How could you, Sophie?' he demanded. 'How could you have done this to me?'

'Fabien, I'm desperately sorry. Please let me explain.'

'What can there be to be explained? Rosine told me everything. It's plain now that you gained my confidence for one reason only. I bared my soul to you that night on the mountain and it was nothing to you but a journalist's scoop.'

She could feel his hands bruising her tender skin, but she did not care.

'Fabien, listen to me. It wasn't like that. If you would just listen to me . . .'

'No, Sophie, it's finished, all finished. Feeling how I do at this moment, I never want to see or hear from you again.'

His hands dropped to his sides and he strode away from her, through the open door and away over the lawns. The golden spaniel ran whimpering after him seeming to sense his mood. Sophie wanted to run after him, to beg, to plead, to explain, but she felt frozen with guilt. There was nothing she could say, nothing that could possibly repair the damage she had done.

CHAPTER ELEVEN

DAYS passed and Sophie saw no one from the château. She seemed to be living a life of isolation, although the village people all knew her by now, and she thought how happy she could have been here in this sunlit country if only things had been different. Vidal was making wonderful progress with the repairs and she had managed to persuade her *notaire* to negotiate a small loan from the bank to buy some materials, but she knew that wouldn't last for long and then she would have to stop the building until she could save for when she could come again. But by that time, Vidal might not be available. He was such a good workman and working for so little. He could easily get some more lucrative job, she felt sure. If only she could afford to buy all the materials so that he could finish it all now!

She did not see Fabien even when she went into the village. Sometimes before when she had gone to market, she had met him, laughing and joking with the people who brought in the vegetables, cheese and honey from their small holdings in the neighbourhood to sell under the tall chestnut trees that dappled the stalls with sunlight. But although she longed yet dreaded to see him again, he was never there. She wondered whether perhaps he had gone away, but Vidal told her he had heard that the old aunt at the château was ill again and she knew he would not leave if that was so. She felt sad not to visit Belle again, but she did not dare to have another confrontation with Fabien.

In her imagination, she could still see him looking down at her, his eyes dark with hatred, and, when he strode away from her, his broad shoulders had seemed to her stiff with dislike. No amount of explanation could put things right, she thought. But did she want to stay here now? Oh, yes, she had learned to love this place. She would have to learn to survive his hatred. When she came here for her infrequent vacations, she need never see him. If she chose, she need never see him again, although there was part of her that longed to have things back as they had been. She remembered how lovely that waltz had been, but that was all in the past now together with that night on the mountain. She must try to forget that she had thought she felt love for him.

She was busying herself over planting an asparagus bed, trying to blot out her gloomy thoughts by some hard labour, when she saw a bright yellow car coming through the trees. Her heart sank as she realised it was Rosine. As usual Rosine was dressed in very flamboyant fashion in a bright red and emerald outfit, of culottes with a bandeau around her breasts that matched the one in her hair.

'Hi, Sophie, I haven't seen you for ages. Why have you been hiding?'

As if she didn't know, thought Sophie.

She accepted a glass of wine from Sophie and sat down on the patio for a chat.

'Affairs are not so good up at the château,' she informed Sophie. 'Poor Belle seems to be fading and Germaine is very *dérangée*. To me it seems without reason, that. One cannot live for ever, *n'est-ce pas?*'

'They must have been together for all their lives,' Sophie remonstrated. 'One can understand she would be upset, and Belle is a charming old lady.'

'Yes, but more than a little mad. She had one love affair in her life and talks as if she had been the greatest courtesan in France.'

'I don't think she does,' Sophie protested. 'She seems to have loved Aristide very deeply.'

'Oh, love,' sneered Rosine, as if dismissing such a thing as a romantic lie. 'But I didn't come here to talk about Belle. What have you done to Fabien? He has gone back to being a hermit. He won't even see me. I am sorry now that I told him about your writing in that English journal. It has done me no good at all.'

'Did you think it would?'

Rosine laughed. Her perfect teeth were diamond-white in the bright red of her mouth and the glossy perfection of her golden skin.

'Of course. It was a very great surprise to me that you, who seemed to be quite the demure English miss, should be a writer and in such an important journal too. It was very clever of you to get that story from Fabien. Did they pay you well for it? Naturally he was furious, but *çela ne fait rien*, so long as they made it worth your while.' She laughed again and her shining dark hair swung back from her head. 'It seems you have offended him deeply. Oh, yes, these de Cressac men have plenty of pride. But soon I think he will see me again and then I will know how to console him.'

'I expect you will,' said Sophie bitterly.

'Don't be displeased with me, dear Sophie. I thought it was all rather a joke. I didn't know Fabien would take it like that, but he is *très sérieux* these days. There was nothing to be ashamed of in that article. I myself thought that you wrote it very well.' She looked slyly sideways at Sophie. 'It sounded almost as if you might be in love with Fabien. Oh, but of course, you have this Mike who came to see you.'

Sophie offered Rosine no explanation, for it didn't seem to be of any use now. Let them think what they would. What did anything matter beside the fact that Fabien hated her?

That evening she had another call from Mike.

'Hi, Sophie, how goes it? It's so near now to the time when you'll be back that I'm holding that cheque for you. Is that all right with you?'

'Perfectly all right, Mike.'

She didn't tell him she didn't want to be paid for it. He would think she was mad. She would give the money to some charity when she got it.

'There's another possibility for an article before you leave.'

'I'm not doing anything personal again, Mike.'

'Nothing personal this time. It's just that you might like

to do an article on the Catharists.'

'And who may they be?' asked Sophie.

'They were the religious fanatics who holed themselves up in the Quéribus château high up on the edge of the Roussillon and threw themselves off the cliff when they could no longer hold out.'

'It sounds charming,' Sophie told him.

'Anyhow, go to Les Corbières and see what you think of it. You'll find it interesting country and, if you can't find enough to trace the history of the Catharists, you could at least do a travel piece. There are some of the best vineyards in France in the Tautauvel area. Oh, and incidentally, will you bring me a couple of dozen bottles of a favourite wine of mine? You'll find the cave where they sell it on the way there.'

'Mike, you are persuading me to go there and do this article just so you can get that wine,' Sophie said suspiciously.

'Well, it will all work in,' he told her airily.

'I don't promise anything, Mike. I'll be coming back very soon and, if it had escaped your memory again, I do happen still to be on leave.'

'That's my girl. Let me give you the address of the cave and the name of the wine. Got that? If you get it for me, you'll be my favourite writer. *Au revoir.*'

Why were all the men she knew so impossible? thought Sophie, exasperated. As if she didn't have enough to worry about without having to go on some wild-goose chase to find wine for Mike. And as for this story about the religious fanatics, it didn't sound at all the kind of story that he would print. It was, as she suspected, he just wanted an excuse to send her to buy wine. Well, she might go and again she might not. She had heard that it was interesting country, quite different from the rest of the Roussillon, but she was not feeling very friendly with Mike after the way he had absconded with her article and led her into so much trouble. But after all, he was her employer. She would have to see what she could do to please him.

A few more days passed. She was getting on so well with clearing the garden and planting various vegetables. She would grow asparagus and artichokes, courgettes and green beans and the tiny broad beans, the kind they call *fèves* in France. One day she might even have an orange-tree though possibly that would need protection in the winter, but she was longing to see ripe golden globes of fruit, glowing against the screen of dark green leaves, as she had seen them in Greece. Perhaps she could employ Pujol to do the garden while she was away in London, for in this dry climate it would probably need watering sometimes. If Mike gave her promotion, as he had promised, she might be able to fly out here once a month.

In this way she tried to think cheerfully of the future and not to dwell on the fact that her association with Fabien was finished. Then one day, when she went to do her shopping, she heard that Belle had died. It had happened some days ago and already the funeral had taken place.

'Why didn't you tell me?' she asked Vidal.

'Pardon, *mademoiselle*, I thought you knew.'

Sophie felt dreadful that she had not known this before and had not got in touch with Germaine. Now she felt she must go to see the old lady, even if it meant having to meet Fabien again. However during the morning he probably wouldn't be there. He seemed to have work on the estate supervising men in the vineyards and winery in the early part of the day. She would have to risk it for she could not put off visiting Germaine to give her condolences. She bought a wreath of freesias and white violets to take to Germaine and drove on the familiar route up to the château.

Germaine was happy to see her and brushed aside her apologies.

'The funeral was a quiet family affair. Belle wished it so. But she spoke of you in those last days. She had taken a great fancy to you, Sophie, and she was particularly pleased that you had worn her dress and she had seen how it could look on someone young once more. She often spoke of the way you and Fabien had danced for her. She liked to think that she had sensed you were in love with him; my poor Belle, she was always a romantic.'

'There was no harm in that,' Sophie told her. 'I found her very charming.'

'Oh, yes, she had very much charm when she was young. Perhaps too much. She was like a beautiful butterfly and Papa guarded her so. The young men flocked around her but Aristide was her one true love. Papa did not approve of her wish to marry a poor artist and, although my brother was so friendly with Aristide, he never succeeded in persuading Papa otherwise. Aristide remained on good terms with Belle all his life. It was only lately that Belle began to fail and hark back to their life together when young.'

'But I think she got a great deal of pleasure from her memories,' Sophie told her.

'Yes, indeed, I suppose it is better to have such memories than none at all.'

Sophie wondered whether Germaine was referring to her own life. She seemed such a rigid person now. Had she ever had a lover? Had she, Sophie wondered, ever felt as she herself had felt that day in the ballroom with Fabien? But she mustn't think of that.

'I would like you to do me one small favour, Sophie,' Germaine announced, and Sophie jerked herself back to the present.

'Anything in my power,' Sophie agreed.

'I'd like you to talk to Fabien. Something, I can't think it is Belle's death, but something has affected him so that he is acting somewhat as he did when he had had a terrible accident some years ago. At that time he withdrew into himself and was deeply depressed. We thought he was getting over it. Lately he has been much more his old self, but now in just the last few days, he seems once more to be plunged into bad moods. He is ill-tempered with his workmen. He hardly speaks at mealtimes and he spends long hours in his room by himself. He does not seem to want to see anyone and refuses to see Rosine.'

'Then I'm quite sure he won't see me,' Sophie declared.

'Maybe not if I ask him,' said Germaine. 'But if you were to go up to his apartment, I could send for him on some pretext and he would have to see you then.'

'He could just tell me to leave,' Sophie suggested.

'No, no,' Germaine told her proudly. 'Fabien is a gentleman. He would never be impolite to a woman.'

Little did she know of men like Fabien, thought Sophie. But if she took this opportunity to meet him, she might be able to put the record straight and this she longed to do. Should she consent to this plan of Germaine's? It was the only chance she could possibly get to explain to Fabien about the ill-fated article.

'Very well,' she told Germaine. 'I'll go up to his apartment, but don't expect miracles. I think I am the last person he wants to see.'

She could see that Germaine didn't believe her. Of course she knew nothing of the cause of Fabien's displeasure. At least this gave Sophie the opportunity she had half longed for, half feared.

She went up the curving staircase and along the picture gallery then into the wing that housed Fabien's apartment. Again the carved dragon glared down at her as if disapproving strongly of her presence here. Should she wait for him in the study? Or would the blue and rose sitting-room provide a more gentle atmosphere for their talk if and when he came? She thought perhaps the boudoir would be kinder to her with its feminine aura and its garlanded hanging of decorative roses.

Opening the door, she paused on the threshold and felt at once struck dumb with astonishment. Leaning against the walls, quite covering the paintings of country scenes that she had seen before, were several large paintings, portraits of a beautiful woman. With surprise she realised that the woman was wearing the very dress that she herself had worn on that day when she had danced with Fabien, and there were other paintings too of the same woman in various stages of undress. These must be the missing pictures! Surely they must be. But what were they doing here?

As she thought about it, she found that she was trembling with rage. How could Fabien have done this to her? When she had looked for the pictures before, he had utterly denied any knowledge of them and now here they were. He must have had them all the time but concealed them because he thought she might see them. Now, when he was sure she would not visit him again, he must have felt safe to bring them out. He had stolen them from her because he did not want her to be able to repair the *mas*, and all the time this was happening, he had been making love to her.

Just as before, she suddenly heard his steps coming firm and strong along the corridor, but now she was too angry to be frightened of his reaction when he saw her. He opened the door and stopped dead on the threshold. He seemed, she thought, to be looking thinner, his dark face gaunt, his eyes lacking their usual fire.

'Sophie,' he said. 'What in the name of heaven are you doing here? I was told someone had something important to say to me. If I had known it was you . . .'

'You would not have come,' Sophie prompted him. 'It's true, I did have something to say to you, but now I have seen these pictures I feel that what I had to say is not important. You asked how I could have written that article, but now I can ask you how could you have deceived me into believing the pictures were missing when all the time you were holding on to them, stealing them from me so I could not realise the money from them, and could not go on with rebuilding the *mas*?

'You wanted the *mas* for yourself and didn't let anything stand in your way to get it, didn't even balk at criminal means to get what you wanted! You, who talked so glibly about the honour of the de Cressacs when all the time these paintings were sitting here! You must have thought it was a good joke that you were making love to me while you were preventing me from getting on with the thing I came here to do, the thing I most wanted to do.'

Under the bronze of his skin, his face showed a greyish pallor. His eyes were alive now, but alive with the fire of his anger. He laughed without humour, mocking laughter that twisted his mobile mouth into an ironic grimace.

'That's very amusing coming from you, Sophie. You deceived me into confession and then broadcast my story to the whole world, and you let me make love to you when all you really wanted from me was that story in order to make money, and now you accuse me of taking the pictures.'

'How can I think otherwise? You have the pictures here. You must have concealed them somewhere when I came before.'

'As I have said before, Sophie, you have a pretty low opinion of me, but the same goes for you. Your actions have not shown you up in a very good light either. However, just to enlighten you, I'll tell you what this is all about, though why I should bother to justify myself to you, I don't know.'

'I discovered the paintings among Belle's belongings. It seems that Aristide gave them to her for safe keeping meaning to let the *notaire* know where they were, but, as you know, Belle was very vague in her mind lately and she had forgotten I think that she had ever had them. They were stuck away in an old cupboard that she never used and with them I found a note from Aristide giving her instructions as to what to do with them when he died. They should have been given back to you when you first came, but by then Belle had forgotten all about them. So that is my criminal act. You can believe me or not as you please, but I'll bring back the pictures tomorrow at the latest and then I think our acquaintance will be closed by mutual consent.'

He strode towards her now and took her face in his hands, then shook his head. Sophie shuddered away from his dark expression.

'What a pity it all is,' he said. 'You are such a lovely woman. What a waste. Goodbye, Sophie. After tomorrow I don't expect to be meeting you ever again.'

CHAPTER TWELVE

SOPHIE had turned and fled away from Fabien, for she felt she could not bear one moment more of his scornful expression turning all his dislike upon her. Of course his story must be true, and she had accused this proud man of being a thief. He would never forgive her now, first for her offence in writing the article about him and now for this wrong accusation. Any attempt at an apology would be more than useless. Oh, why had she accused him so wildly, why couldn't she have waited for his explanation of the presence of the paintings in his room?

He had said he would bring the paintings tomorrow, but she couldn't face meeting him once more. She would do as Mike had asked and go to Les Corbières to buy his wine, for soon she would have to leave here and resume her ordinary life. She supposed that now she would be able to sell the paintings, maybe at Collioure where she had met the dealer, but she did not know whether she wanted the *mas* to be finished. It had too many unhappy memories for her.

Yes, tomorrow, when Fabien came with the pictures, she was determined she would not be there. She would ask Vidal to receive them for her but she herself would be far away. She got out her road map and studied it carefully. She would go across Roussillon to the extreme edge past Thuir to where there were these other mountains.

Once more she could not sleep, but this time she was wary of taking a sleeping-pill. A nightingale sang in the orchard, its song as piercingly sweet as the notes of the *cobla* on that day when she had gone up the mountain with Fabien. He could not think any worse of her now and yet she longed to set the record straight. She thought it really was not much use now to attempt an explanation about the article, and yet she could not bear it that he thought she was so utterly mercenary as to make use of his confession in that way.

She wandered into the living-room unable to settle and then it came to her that she would write a letter and try to explain what had happened. She need not see him or engage in any argument. Maybe he would tear the letter up without even reading it, but chances were that he would be curious to find out what she had to say. She would leave it with Vidal and he could give it to Fabien when he brought the paintings.

Next day she waited for Vidal to come and explained that she intended driving to Les Corbières and to buy wine in the Tautauvel region.

'Quite a long drive that,' Vidal commented. 'But certainly there they know how to make good wine. You will be able to see the castle of Peyrepertuse and the Quéribus château while you are there. It's worth seeing high on the mountain and there's the gorge of Calamus too. Oh, yes, it's worth a visit though it's rugged country, not as soft as these parts.'

'I intend to go to Peyrepertuse,' she told him, 'after I've bought the wine. Is it very rough country?'

'Not particularly. The roads are good if winding. The country is wild but you'll get there all right without any trouble.'

She stopped in the village to get some provisions for she thought she would take a picnic lunch. She had bought a baguette and cheese, ham and fruit when she met Rosine also doing her shopping. She was wearing bright blue Bermuda shorts and a clinging shocking-pink top and was looking very cheerful.

'Hi, Sophie, *comment ça va*? How goes it? I'm glad to tell

you that Fabien welcomed me to the château last night. I thought he would get tired of his own company sooner or later. What an amusing thing that dear old Belle had your paintings hidden away all the time! Germaine is most put out that she had unintentionally deprived you of them. Seems to think she has stained the honour of the de Cressacs by not knowing what Belle has been up to, but I'm sure you can put her straight on that. Fabien wouldn't even discuss the pictures with me. He got quite angry when I spoke of them. He is such a sensitive man, although he is so virile.'

He was probably so angry with her still over the matter of the pictures that he didn't want to have any further discussion even with Rosine. It was a wonder she had not wormed out of him the fact that Sophie had suspected him of stealing them.

She drove away trying to fight off the thought that Fabien had quickly found consolation with Rosine. She was sure her letter would do no good. She had sinned in two respects. Not only had she written the article about him betraying his intimate confidence but now she had unjustly suspected him of stealing her pictures. She had offended him in that most sensitive area, his pride. And none of this had been intended, yet she knew he would never forgive her.

As she was thinking these gloomy thoughts, she was driving her little car swiftly and competently across country as if she were trying to get away from everything that had happened to her in the last weeks. She would buy the wine for Mike, have a look at this part of the country and then tomorrow she would make preparations for her return to London. She did not think she would ever want to come here again. Let Fabien have the *mas* now. She felt she wanted to finish it all for good, to forget those moments of bliss when he had made love to her, to forget the passionate response she had felt to his kisses. It was all ended now and it had meant very little to him. He had gone back to Rosine if he had ever left her in the first place.

It was a strange country in which she found herself. In the distance mountains towered above the valleys where vines grew row upon row receding into the distance. Olive trees and oaks clung to the lower slopes but above that there seemed to be a landscape of stones and pinnacles of rock. She stopped at one of the caves where wine was sold. She had been instructed as to what wine she should purchase so she refused the samples of wine that the jovial propietor wanted to press upon her. She must keep a clear head for driving.

'*Vous êtes Britannique?*' he asked, and shook his head that such a beautiful girl should be travelling alone.

She asked about Peyrepertuse and he told her the way to go.

'You will see the château. Its ruins are high on the mountain looking like the rocks themselves. They were clever, our ancestors, to manage to build on so high a pinnacle. But these valleys were not always peaceful as they are now. Lying between France and Spain, the wars flowed across this land. That is why there are citadels on the mountain tops, between the sky and the valleys.'

As she drove on Sophie thought that the villages seemed to be the warm colour of the sun and the rocks of which they were built. Tall, dark cypresses seemed to lend them dignity crowding around the little churches.

But in her present state of mind she wanted to get away from people and she drove over the winding road higher and higher above the valley until the distant ridge of mountains became clear and indistinctly she could see the outlines of the ruined château high overhead looking for all the world as if it had grown out of the rocks themselves. Now the road had come directly underneath and there was nowhere to drive further.

She got out of her car and gazed up at the wild scene above her. There was a path winding steeply upwards and she began to make her way up, feeling that it would be good to be somewhere far away from her present troubles, a place where she could stand on top of the world and feel herself free of the desperate emotions that were plaguing her.

She made her way up, scrambling over boulders and feeling rather breathless, but at last she had arrived at the top. She was quite alone and now she could see that the grim remains of the château stood in ruins over the topmost ridge of the mountain. The walls and ledges were, she thought, of sandstone built in irregular blocks. There were piles of stones where there had been buildings but still some turrets were left.

She entered a round tower by a small doorway and, looking through the slit window, she saw below her the whole of the valley with its winding roads and mountains beyond. Over there was Quéribus, the last refuge of those Catharists about whom Mike had spoken. It was on top of a seemingly unscalable peak and she wondered how he could possibly have expected her to go there. He obviously didn't know the lie of the land, for it stood high on a jagged pinnacle of rock as high as or higher than the place on which she stood.

She had brought a haversack with her and now she ate her *déjeuner* and lay on a sun-warmed flat rock sheltered from the wind by one of the old walls. She thought how happy she could have been in this country of the Roussillon, so varied in its scenery, from the high peaks of the Pyrenees, the snow-covered Canigou to the shining foam of the Mediterranean sea with all the lovely valleys between, the green vineyards, the foaming blossom of the orchards. But it was not for her now.

She had missed much of her rest the night before and

soon in the pleasant heat of the afternoon sun, that was
cooled by the mountain breeze, she fell into a deep sleep.
When she awoke, the sun was lower in the sky and she
found she had slept for a long time. Her limbs ached from
their contact with the hard face of the rock and for a
moment she could not remember how she had got there.
She felt giddy and her legs trembled as she rose, ready to
undertake the steep downward journey. She wondered
whether there was any other way less precipitous where she
could find her way off the mountain and she wandered
around still not feeling quite awake as she sought it. She was
standing on the edge of a rocky place looking down, when
suddenly her feet slipped from under her on the crumbling
stones and she screamed as she felt herself hurtling into
space.

The shock must have made her lose consciousness for a
moment, and when she came to she found herself on a
narrow ledge with steep rock face above her and a drop of
thousands of metres below. She shuddered as she realised
her position. She was bruised and scratched and one ankle
felt as if it had been twisted but the scrub growing all
around must have broken her fall. But how was she to get
back?

She looked at the rock face above her. It was smooth as
glass from the weathering of the elements and, where she
tried to grasp it, large pieces broke off and fell with a dull
sound somewhere far away below her. She looked
desperately around her. There had been no one here all day
except herself, and now that the sun was low in the sky it
was hardly likely that anyone would come here. How many
visitors came to this place? she wondered. At this time of
year it was hardly the high season for tourists. It could be
days before anyone saw her here.

There were not even any cars on the looping roads
below. Ah, yes, there was a car like a little silver beetle

scurrying on its way, but it was too far away for the driver to see her. She had never felt so helpless before. She made one attempt to start climbing the face but was beaten back by the sheer impossibility of it. She dared not look below her where birds were circling in the clear air or being borne aloft on the breezes of evening. Suppose a storm should come up in the night? Sophie remembered how quickly the weather had changed that time on the mountain with Fabien. How foolish she had been to come here alone. She had not realised the dangers.

She crouched there on her narrow ledge feeling more and more aching as the full extent of her bruises developed. If a wind came up she had nothing with which to tie herself even if there had been a rock handy. But all around her was smooth. There was not even a rock to which she could cling.

The sun was setting now, filling all the valley with its glory of gold and flame but the limestone crags around her looked even more serrated and menacing and the dark jagged outline of the château seemed to deny that anything human had ever been able to survive there. And then she heard it, the sound of stones falling away from someone's footsteps. At first she thought she was imagining it. Maybe it was the wind disturbing the small rocks on the high exposed ridges, but no, it could be footsteps and hopefully she began to shout,

'*Au secours,*' she shouted as loudly as she could. 'Help, help!'

The sound ceased and she held her breath then shouted again. Again she heard the sound of steps crunching over the rocks.

'Sophie,' she heard a voice shout, 'is that you? Where the devil are you?'

With an immense thrill of recognition, she knew the voice belonged to Fabien.

'I'm here below you,' she shouted. 'I've fallen and I can't

get back.'

She saw him clearly now peering over the edge and, at his side, Vidal of all people.

'How did you know I was here?' she asked weakly.

'Never mind about that now. We'll need a rope for this. Vidal must go back for one. I have one in the boot of my car. Vidal, be as quick as you can. Are you all right, Sophie?'

'I think so. My ankle's a bit twisted and I'm badly bruised but otherwise I'm fine unless you count being terrified over the drop below me and completely unable to climb up there.'

'But I can climb down,' Fabien said and he straightaway lowered himself over the edge.

'No, don't do it,' Sophie screamed as she saw him coming down over seemingly impossible hand-holds. 'You should have waited for the rope,' she panted. 'I thought you were going to be killed.'

'And would you have cared?' he asked.

She flung herself into his arms and they swayed together on the narrow ledge.

'Good grief, Sophie, do you want to kill us both?'

She was ashamed to have shown her feelings so openly to him as he set her down and crouched beside her. Looking at his proud profile she could not tell what he might be thinking. He was probably blaming her for getting them into this situation. He did not speak but she felt his hands go around her shoulders and she felt protected from the horrible depths below her.

There was a shout from above and Vidal appeared with a rope in his hand.

'I can tie it to this rock,' he cried. 'But I'll have to hold it too. I doubt whether it can take both of you.'

'It doesn't have to,' Fabien told him. 'I will rope Sophie and bring her up on my back, then if I should fall, she will still be safe. You should be able to take her weight.'

'No, Fabien, you can't do that.' Sophie protested. 'It's impossible to climb this face. I've tried. It's smooth as ice.'

'You seem to forget that I was used to climbing on ice. Don't argue, Sophie. This is one area in which you must trust me, even if you can't believe in me otherwise.'

He tied the rope around her securely then hoisted her on his back like a child being given a ride by an adult and, in this situation, it was true she felt as ignorant as a child would have been. Then slowly he began the dangerous climb up the face. At times his foot slipped and loose rock clattered down the side of the mountain as her heart seemed to stop beating. Below her the whole vast valley swung in dizzying glimpses and she closed her eyes and tried to concentrate only on his nearness, the hardness of the muscles of his back pressed against the softness of her breasts as she clung to him, the warmth of his body under her hands.

She expected that at any moment he would lose his footing and be dashed to pieces on the jagged rocks below, and she herself would be left swinging like a pendulum in space. But then Vidal could rescue her, but she dared not think what would happen to her then for she knew that without him her life would be as good as over. She knew now that whatever he felt for her, she truly loved him. She had realised this when she had seen him making his way towards her over the treacherous face.

They were near the top now with Vidal shouting encouragement and holding tightly to the rope, and now they were there, safe at last. Her legs were so weak she collapsed on the ground and tears rained down her face as she sobbed aloud.

'I know you hate tears, Fabien, but this time you'll have to endure them,' she gasped.

He raised her up in his arms and held her close so that she

seemed to feel the strength of him flowing into her.

'No tears are needed now, Sophie. You have helped me to find myself again. This time I had no fear. My only thought was for you. Give Vidal the keys of your car. He can go on ahead and drive your car home. You are coming with me.'

She was glad of his support as they slowly came down the mountain path for she was still weak and trembling, and when at last they were seated safe in the little silver car, she turned to him and asked again, 'How was it you came here?'

'I came to the *mas* with the paintings, meaning to have a talk with you, but you had gone and Vidal gave me the letter and told me where you had gone. I believe you, Sophie, that you didn't mean it should be published but also I read the article that Rosine had brought to me. I realise now that there was no harm in it. Quite the contrary in fact. Once and for all it vindicated me in the eyes of the world, and it told me something else too.'

'What was that?' Sophie asked.

'It told me that you love me. At least that is the interpretation I put on it. Can that be true, Sophie?'

'Yes, it's true,' she told him sadly. 'I know it now but I guess it's too late. You can never forgive me for all the mistakes and misunderstandings that have happened since we met.'

'Never too late,' he said. 'Never too late for love. Oh, Sophie, I think I have loved you since the first moment I saw you wrapped in that rose-coloured towel and so highly indignant with me that your red hair seemed to give off sparks. This Mike, will he mind very much that I am going to take you away from him, that he is going to lose Sophie, his most talented journalist?'

'*Cela ne fait rien*. It doesn't matter what Mike thinks,' Sophie told him.

'That's good, because now I know I can never let you go.

As soon as we can manage it, you are going to be Sophie, my most talented and loving wife.'

'And will I be allowed to finish the *mas?*'

'*Bien sûr*, of course, we will need somewhere to go away from the château somewhere to be completely alone, somewhere to make love. We must put that splendid bed to it's proper use, *n'est-ce pas?*'

'*M. le Comte,* you are incorrigible,' said Sophie, before he stopped her protest with a kiss.

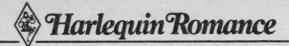
Harlequin Romance

Coming Next Month

2887 LOVE'S PERJURY Mariana Francis
Diana makes a deathbed promise to her sister, Kris, to raise
Kris's baby son. But David Farnham thinks Diana is the mother
of his brother's child . . . a lie she prays he will go on believing.

2888 THE CHAUVINIST Vanessa Grant
Kristy can't believe her ears when, within hours of meeting
Blake Harding again, he calmly informs her she's going to
marry him. But she hasn't forgotten his rejection twelve years
ago, and neither has Blake.

2889 TEMPORARY PARAGON Emma Goldrick
When Beth Murphy set out to avenge her niece's reputation,
she discovers how difficult it is to arrange a wedding.
Particularly when the intended groom is more intent on
marrying Beth.

2900 AUTUMN AT AUBREY'S Miriam MacGregor
Donna's visit to a resort in New Zealand's Lake Taupo region is
anything but a holiday. Especially when the arrogant resort
owner expects her to pretend to be his lover to ward off
his ex-wife!

2901 THE DOUBTFUL MARRIAGE Betty Neels
Matilda is more than surprised at Doctor Rauward van
Kempler's proposal, but but she sensibly agrees to the marriage
of convenience—only to find herself far from sensibly
involved.

2902 ENTRANCE TO EDEN Sue Peters
When Kay's culinary talents are doubted by a handsome
aristocrat who hires her to cater a wedding, she vows to prove
him wrong and be done with him. But he seems intent on
having her around. . . .

Available in January wherever paperback books are sold, or
through Harlequin Reader Service.

In the U.S.
901 Fuhrmann Blvd.
P.O. Box 1397
Buffalo, N.Y. 14240-1397

In Canada
P.O. Box 603
Fort Erie, Ontario
L2A 5X3

Harlequin Intrigue

In October
Watch for the new look of

Harlequin Intrigue

...because romance can be quite an adventure!

Each time, Harlequin Intrigue brings you great stories, mixing a contemporary, sophisticated romance with the surprising twists and turns of a puzzler...romance with "something more."

Plus...
in next month's publications of Harlequin Intrigue we offer you the chance to win one of four mysterious and exciting weekends. Don't miss the opportunity! Read the October Harlequin Intrigues!

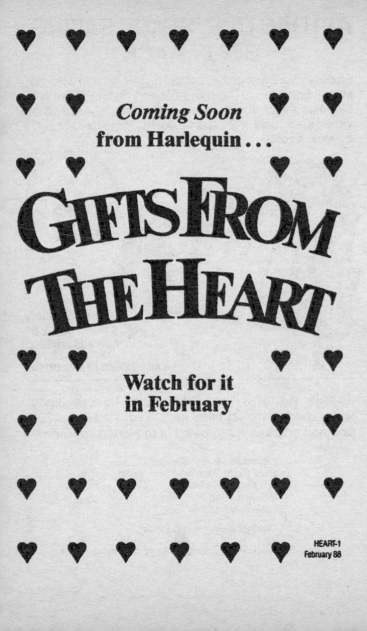

Coming Soon
from Harlequin . . .

GIFTS FROM THE HEART

Watch for it
in February

HEART-1
February 88

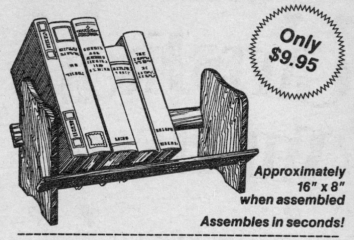